About the Author

Tom Scantlebury wanted to become an author for most of his life, and if not an author, he'd be just as happy running about as a Time Lord, or maybe a pirate. He lives in London, where he divides his time between writing, going to the theatre and spending far too much money on books.

The Missing God

Tom Scantlebury

The Missing God

Olympia Publishers
London

www.olympiapublishers.com
OLYMPIA PAPERBACK EDITION

A CIP catalogue record for this title is
available from the British Library.

ISBN: 978-1-80074-670-1

First Published in 2023

Olympia Publishers
Tallis House
2 Tallis Street
London
EC4Y 0AB

Printed in Great Britain

Dedication

To Gramps. My loudest supporter, from the very beginning.

Acknowledgements

Thank you to all at Olympia, the people who made my dream of one day being published come true. To everyone who worked on this book, to get it from my head into the hands of readers, you have my unending thanks! To all at Team H – Jess A, Freddie C, Harry C, Gina F, Martha H, Rebeca L, Olivia R, Sarah L, Emma L, Kaylee H, Des B, Ellie H, Patrick G, Isabel M, Rama U, James R, Joe P, Joe J, Lou F, Elsie O, Anita N, Harry CB, Tony F, Ralph O, Alex R, Hope B and Ryan C. To all at Team G – Rebecca B, Zoe D, Zoe M, Peter S, Andy W, Jo R, Sylvia G, Faruk A, Victoria V, Robyn K, Luke C, Simao R, Rianna G, Jess B, Tom B, Hannah M, Louise N, Charlie BC, Rachael B, Becky H, Richard ED and Jenny CW. To CHF, who believed I could write a book – looks like you were right all along! To my Managers Extraordinaire – Adam E, Gail D, Alex C, Mark S, Mark H, Mark S, Naim M, Jeff N, Sue M, Joseph W, Echina E, Martin S, Christina H, Sarah P, Ella P and Elizabeth S. To the wonderful Team T – Tania C, Amy Y, Em B, Naoise N, Josh B, Steven H, Ashley B, Sally F, Charlotte F, Anna PH, Elliot S, Kwami C, Alice B and Will P and Sean B, you guys rock! (And yes, I'll make sure I sign the book for you!) To Team LTD – Georgie H, Roger O, Angus C, Pauline D, Caley P, James F and Temuri S, you guys really are brilliant! To Team S – Steve, Claire, Anna, Zoe, Michelle, Trefor, Hannah, Derek, Pat, Emma, Rebecca, Drew, Emily, Matt, Charlie, Dan, Glyn, Gill, Claire, Fay and

Richard. To Team C – Terry, Barry, Carol, Kevin, Kate, Lou, Nicola, Jason, Jordanna, Bradley, Megan, Logan, Jason, Lewis, Abbie, Charlie, Lucy, Tommy, Jack, Ollie, Freddie, Joe, Riley, Leah, Charlotte, Charlie, Alfie, Teddie, Rachelle, Jess, and Adam. To my grandparents, for all their support. To my Exceptional Eight – Howard J, Ruthie P, Freddie C, Jess A, Rebecca B, Em F, Charlotte H and Johnny Y – you guys have all my heart, always. I love you so much. To my brother, who is, actually, rather awesome. To my parents, for everything. And to you, for picking up this book, and giving Seb, Frankie, Levi, Clara and me a chance. Thank you.

Chapter One
Seb

There's not much in the world that scares me.

Growing up with an adventurer for a mother – Mum always said *adventurer*, never 'travel writer' – had seen me face down tidal waves, death-drops from cliffs and jungles so dense it felt like we'd never get out. I doubted there was anything left in the world that could give me a fright.

But this nightmare was certainly trying.

It had started like a normal dream. Or at least, it had started like what I thought a normal dream would be. I'd been standing alone in a banqueting hall, the kind you'd find in an old castle, with long tables and tall chairs that had been made out of dark wood, each with a different symbol carved along the back. Behind the chairs was a huge fireplace, where a fire made up of different coloured flames was dancing away in the grate. At the far end of the room on a raised platform were twelve golden thrones, all marked with different carvings, and all empty.

I'd had dreams like this before, usually after Mum and Ma had dragged me to a museum for a day out. Dreams where I'd walk about in some empty old castle, imagining I owned the place. Maybe this would be just like them. I took a few steps forward towards the golden thrones, my eyes on the carvings across each of them. The throne in the middle of the line-up was the biggest, with an eagle carved across it, with its wings touching each of the arm rests and its body across the back of the chair. If I sat in the throne, the eagle would have been completely hidden from view. As I got nearer, it became clear that the bird's wings were made up of bright red rubies, and its eyes were emeralds. I reached out my hand, letting my fingers run across the sharp rubies. Then things got weird. Really weird.

Without warning, the roof of the banqueting hall was ripped clean off and tossed aside like paper. The flames in the grate spluttered and died away, the wind cutting through them. I spun round and came face to face with...

I blinked. There was no way what I was seeing was real.

Looming over the hall was a Cyclops. It had one giant green eye, which was staring down at me. It was taller than anything I'd ever seen, and its body was bulging in all the wrong places, like it had broken apart and put back together too quickly.

"Mortal!" the Cyclops called, venomously. "The mortal is here!"

I recoiled back as it screamed. This guy really needed to invest in some mouthwash.

The Cyclops leaned down, trying to get a better look at me. As it moved, I caught sight of hundreds of arrows sticking out of its body. Where they had hit, a bright blue liquid was oozing out and dripping onto the floor below.

"How are you still alive?" I called, although why I was choosing to make conversation with the Cyclops and not run for my life, I don't know.

The Cyclops moved in closer, its hand outstretched, ready to snatch me up. I winced as its terrible breath invaded my nostrils again. The Cyclops was inches away from me. Even if I tried to escape, it would be pointless. He only had to reach his hand out, and I'd be caught. There was nothing I could do.

"RUN!"

From out of nowhere, a man had appeared. He was wearing

heavy, golden armour and had long, flowing blonde hair. He was aiming a bow and arrow at the Cyclops, stood directly in front of me. I stared at him, trying to work out where he had come from.

"Are you deaf?" he roared at me. "I said run!"

This time, I did as he said. I took off at a run, tearing out of the banqueting hall as the Cyclops let out a scream of fury.

"APOLLO!" the Cyclops screamed. "How dare you interrupt my hunt! I shall kill you for this!"

As I turned the corner out of the banqueting hall, I heard the man, Apollo, let out a laugh.

"When have you ever been able to kill me?" he laughed. I thought it was a bit stupid, laughing in the face of a screaming and angry Cyclops, but I didn't have time to tell Apollo that. I had to focus on getting out of here, and quickly.

As I ran, I heard what sounded like the whizz of arrows flying through the air, and another scream from the Cyclops. I guess Apollo had hit his mark. I kept running, my head down, my legs moving with a speed I had never had before, my feet eventually feeling something other than the hard floor of the banqueting hall. Something like smooth stone, but even softer, like clouds. At some point, I had made it outside into—

That was *not* possible.

I'd expected to run out into the grounds of a castle, or an estate. I had not expected to run out into the most beautiful city I had ever seen. I was greeted by the sight of buildings made of polished gold and silver, and even the road under my feet sparkled like diamonds. In the distance there was a large amphitheatre, and beyond that a magnificent palace made of polished white marble. There were elegant braziers lining the streets, all with roaring fires lit in them. Overhead, stars illuminated the night sky, each one sparking brighter than the last.

It would have been beautiful, if the entire city was not being attacked by monsters.

"We got in!" I leapt into the shadow of a golden doorway as two giants, both scarred and bleeding, stormed past me, their clubs raised in their fat fists.

"We got in! We got in! We got in!" they repeated, like a football chant. They swayed, and as they passed me, I saw that their legs were, like the monster back in the banqueting hall, covered with arrows. As the giants' shadows passed over me, I dared to look at where they had come from.

Big mistake. Huge mistake. The biggest mistake I could have made.

There were even more monsters pouring in, through two smashed up gates that looked like they might have been gold once upon a time. Now, they were a mixture of dust, ash and what looked like blood.

Monster after monster – more giants, a great buffalo with its head turned down and a creature that could not decide between the body of a man or a wolf, were charging forward, while a giant golden eagle swooped down, clawing at them.

"Defend the Gods!" the eagle cried out in a clear voice.

Out of everything that I'd seen in this nightmare, it was the eagle talking that freaked me out the most.

"Protect the Palace of Olympus!" the eagle screeched, plummeting towards the oncoming onslaught of monsters, its sharp talons outstretched. "Do not let them in!"

Too late for that, I thought. The gates of the city were being trampled on by giants whose feet were the sizes of double-decker buses. There was no chance of keeping them out. From overheard, there came another, more desperate shout.

"Lord Zeus has fled Olympus! Fall back! Fall back my

brethren! Back!"

I looked up, and saw the most muscular man I'd ever seen. His entire body was made of muscle, and in his hand he carried a massive sword. He looked like he'd lost a few fights, his face a mess of blood and cuts, but his eyes were full of anger. He was clinging onto a flying horse, it's wings as white as snow, and its eyes as red as fire.

"Fall back! I order you to fall back!" he bellowed at the fighters below. "We cannot win! As God of War, I order you to retreat!"

Whatever was happening, it was not going well for him.

"What the…"

Before I could finish his sentence, another beast had appeared from beyond the gates. This one, like the wolf-man before it, couldn't decide on a form. It flickered between a long, emerald green snake the size of a few houses, or a dragon, with thick green scales and sharp teeth bared in a sick grin. Its nostrils were smoky and bloody – it could only be blood – was dripping from its open mouth. It slithered to its fullest height in dragon form, and let out a hiss, its beady eyes trained on a golden chariot which was circling above the city, pulled by what had to be invisible horses. Apollo, his hair flying in his face, was at the reigns of the chariot, one hand steering, the other holding a solid gold bow.

"Python!" Apollo yelled, his voice light, as if he were trying not to laugh. "Fancy round two?"

He loosed an arrow, and it hit the dragon-snake creature straight in the neck. I'd played enough Call of Duty to know that shots to the neck usually meant your opponent was finished, but evidently those rules did not apply to Python, who simply shook himself off and carried on slithering forward, aiming his forked tongue at Apollo. From behind him, there was movement as a cackling old woman with sharp teeth and blazing eyes appeared, flying wingless above the city, missing Apollo's chariot by inches.

"The mortal is here!" she screeched, her voice high and reedy. "The mortal boy has been found! Seize him, before the gods can use him for their plans! Seize the boy!"

I looked straight into the eyes of this flying woman, and knew at once that she was talking about me. She was grinning like she'd been handed a winning lottery ticket and swooped down, her claw-like hands ready to seize me up.

I took off running like my life depended on it, which I guess it did. I tore past more monsters, ducking in and out of shadows, under the loincloths of Cyclopes (would not recommend it) until I finally managed to find shelter away from the battle in an abandoned building. I heard the frustrated scream of the wingless woman, who was furiously banging and scratching on the door. I backed as far away as I could, certain that she would get in. The building was made of the blackest stone I had ever seen, as if someone had burned each stone individually and placed them here. Even the flames coming from the small brazier were black. I could still hear the battle raging outside, and the door didn't look like it could take much more beating from the woman outside. There was nowhere else for me to run. I'd trapped myself, and any minute now, she would get in and tear me apart. The door buckled and flew off, slamming into the floor. I went to run, hoping against hope she'd let me go—

She wasn't there. There was no one beyond the door. Even the sound of the battle had died away, leaving an eerie silence.

"Well, that was fun."

I spun round, and nearly screamed. The building had been

totally empty when I came in, but now, there was another man inside. Through the light now streaming in from where the door had been, I could see it was a sort of library, with row upon row of bookcases lined up with dusty old books.

He had long black hair tied in a ponytail, and his pale face was illuminated by the sunlight streaming in. He was wearing entirely black, from his shirt to his trainers. The only thing about him that was bright were his eyes, which were the brightest blue I had ever seen.

"Who—" I began.

"No," he cut in. "No names. Say your name with that lot around," he indicated where the woman had been banging on the door, "and you're in trouble."

His voice was low and urgent, and he kept glancing past me towards the doorway.

"We have very little time before my brothers bring the battle back this way," he continued. "Listen very carefully to what I am about to tell you. I have been allowed to cross into your dreams, to access the power of Morpheus in order to deliver a warning."

He spoke even faster, as if he was on some invisible timer. From outside, the sounds of the battle started to get louder again.

"What you are seeing is real. It is not a dream or a nightmare. It is happening. By the time you wake up, it will have happened many years ago," he said. Like that made any sense. "We need you. Me and my family will need you. You must find the missing god."

Without warning, the man doubled over and dropped to his knees. I went to help him up, but he held out a hand to stop me. "I do not know where he is, or who has taken him, but it has been foretold that a mortal will be the one to find him. You must find Zeus, and you must do it soon, or we will all be damned!"

The man was panting and groaning in pain, his entire body twisted. With a final cry of 'find him!' he vanished, and the world around me, the magnificent buildings, Apollo and his arrows, the man in black and the monsters that had chased me fell away, leaving me alone as the sky turned black and the stars began to fall.

I woke up, panting and drenched in sweat, my red hair sticking to my forehead. Sitting bolt upright, I switched on my bedside lamp and groped around for my phone. Switching it on, I saw the time. 4.22 a.m. I groaned, switching the torch on my phone on, and shining it around. My room looked exactly how it had when I'd gone to bed.

Bedside table? Check.

Two wardrobes? Check.

Writing desk? Check.

Mountains of clothes on the floor? Check.

Band posters all over the wall? Check.

The one nearest to me was new. Mum had brought it for me along with the band's new album, which sat beside the turntable on my desk.

THE BOY AND HIS MUSES

'FOR A MUSE OF FIRE'

The poster showed the band – nine dark skinned women, all with a variety of instruments, and the lead singer, a young blonde-haired guy – stood in front of a ruined temple. I took one last look and went to switch off my torch, when something caught my eye.

I got up, my feet making contact with the soft carpet, and walked towards the poster, avoiding the bundle of uncompleted homework on the floor.

I was staring at the poster for THE BOY AND HIS MUSES, my eyes on the lead singer. Harry Jones looked like he was in his twenties, and was handsome, with tanned skin and bright eyes. He was one of most popular singers around, and was always in the newspapers, usually because he was dating some film star or supermodel. But looking at him now, after that nightmare, something made me feel uneasy. The more I looked at him, the more I realised he looked exactly like Apollo had in my dream. Not just a little bit of a resemblance, like when people say I look like Ron Weasley because I've got red hair and a few freckles. We're talking exactly the same person. Same face, same hair, same everything.

I brought my phone up to the poster and snapped a photo of it. I didn't know what I was going to do with the photo, but it felt important to have it. I was just about to switch my torch off, when something moved.

Something else was here.

"Hello?" I called out, making sure I was quiet enough to stop the rest of the house waking up, passing my torch over each part of the room. "Who's there?"

Nothing. No movement, no sound, nothing.

I shook the thought off. I was just freaked out by my dream, that was all. That was why I thought Apollo looked like Harry Jones. I was just freaked out.

I went back to bed, switching my torch off and willed my mind to let me sleep and not show me dreams of monsters and flying women with claws.

The strangest thing – and there had been a few strange things so far – was that as my eyes closed, I was sure I heard someone in the room whisper something that sounded like, 'It's worked! Contact with the mortal has been established!'

And even weirder, I'm sure it was the voice of Apollo.

Thankfully, when I woke up, I didn't find anyone in my room except me. I tried to push the thoughts of my dream out of my head, but every now and then as I got ready for school, my eyes would wander over to the poster of The Boy and His Muses and I would think back to the sight of Apollo fighting Python. As I was getting dressed, an idea sprang into my mind. I grabbed hold of my Maths books and flipped to the back page. I'd already covered it in bored doodles and sketches, but this was much more important than some bored pieces of art. I found a clean page and jotted down what I remembered from my nightmare.

1 *There was a city that was under attack by monsters*

2 *One of the monsters was called Python*

3 *Apollo had been there. He looks exactly like Harry Jones from Muses.*

4 *There was a man dressed in black*

5 *Something about a missing god?*

I thought back. I knew Apollo was a Greek god, but that didn't explain why he'd been in my dream, or why he looked like Harry Jones.

"Seb! You awake?"

Mum's voice jolted me back to reality. It was half seven. I had precisely twenty minutes before Frankie Sibanda, my best friend since I was three days old, would pull up in her Dad's car and we'd make the journey to school together, just like we did every day. It had been our routine since we'd started at secondary school last year. Mr Sibanda, Frankie's dad, would drive us to school, and Ma would drive us home.

That's when the thought hit me.

Clara.

Clara Liu had become friends with me and Frankie in our

first year, and she was obsessed with Greek myths! If there was anyone I could ask about my dream, and why Apollo looked like Harry Jones, it would be Clara!

I bounded out of my room and downstairs, actually excited to get to school. (No, I can't believe I wrote that either).

"Someone's happy!" Ma said from the kitchen. The smell of freshly baked bread and warm tea made my stomach grumble.

"What happened, did you think up a new excuse for not doing your homework?" Mum asked, sternly.

Oh, I probably should explain that I have two Mums.

Mum – Liz to everyone else – is the travel writer. She's got long brown hair and can be super stern. Ma – Dot – has the reddest hair I've ever seen, and is the kind of Ma that would tell you off for skiving off school and then suggest going to cinema to watch a film. They couldn't be more different, but that's what makes them so perfect together.

"No," I said, helping myself to a slice of toast from the table, "I just woke up in a good mood!"

That's a lie! my brain said. *You woke up nearly screaming in fright!*

I silently told my brain to shut up and polished off the rest of my toast. My younger brother Ben was happily colouring over Mum's latest article for The Weekly Traveller, the travel magazine Mum had created with her best friend, my aunt Anne. I did not want to be here when Mum found out that the article she'd spent three weeks writing now looked like a Jackson Pollock painting.

"Is Mae not up yet?" I asked. Mae was my younger sister, in her final year at my old primary school. She had bright red hair like me, and Mum always said we were two peas in a pod.

"Not yet," Ma said, taking a gulp of tea. "I did ask Raf to

wake her up, but no joy."

"He's probably still doing his hair," I smirked. Raf was my older brother, and in Year 11. He, unlike me, had Mum's brown hair, and it had to be absolutely perfect before he left the house. And yes, I did wind him up about that. Every day.

From outside, a car horn cut through the air.

"That's Frankie," I said, grabbing my school bag. "See you later!" I allowed Mum and Ma to kiss me on the cheek, and gave Ben a high-five as I left the kitchen and made my way to the door.

Considering how the morning had started, with nightmares about Greek gods and monsters, I was feeling pretty positive. My plan was simple. Get to school, ask Clara about the Greek myths and if there had ever been a fight on Mount Olympus, and have her tell me it happened centuries ago and I was probably just dreaming about it because we'd been looking at Greek myths in English.

What could possibly go wrong?

Chapter Two
Frankie

"FRANCESCA SIBANDA! GET DOWN HERE! WE ARE NOT WAITING FOR YOU ANY LONGER!"

Sigh.

Monday morning and Dad was already on my case. I tried not to grumble as I pulled my school jumper over my head and shoved the last of my school provisions – pencil case, calculator, phone and bottle of Coke – into my bag. I didn't see what the problem was. We'd still be waiting for Rosie anyway. It took her longer to get ready than most supermodels.

"Coming Dad!" I called, taking one last look around my room to make sure I had everything. As I made my way downstairs, I could still hear Rosie in her room, singing along off-key to the latest Taylor Swift song. I threw open the door to her room and was greeted by the usual smell of her perfume.

"Get out!" she huffed, getting up to push me towards the door. She was wearing the same uniform as me, but looked about a hundred times more cool.

"Hurry up! Dad's been ready to go for ages!" I said before she could shut the door again.

"It's not even half-seven!" Rosie complained. "Most people aren't even awake yet!"

"We are not most people," Mum chimed from her office. I hadn't realised the door was open, but after hearing her voice, I went and leaned against the doorframe. Mum and me could not have looked more different if we tried. Whereas Dad and I had the same caramel coloured skin, the same black hair and the same dark brown eyes, Mum was pale with brown hair and green eyes. Dad always said her eyes reminded him of the sea. I thought they looked more like the kind of green that made up broccoli, but I never said so. Mum's office was a mismatch of flowers, some in vases, some in boxes and some just laying across her desk, but she always said that was the price she paid for agreeing to take over the florists where she worked.

"Don't give your sister so much grief." Mum smiled at me, her Irish accent as strong as it was when she moved to England twenty years ago. "You know why, she wants to look good," I tutted.

It was so like Mum to take Rosie's side. Just because Rosie had snagged herself a boyfriend last year, it didn't mean she had to take hours to get ready.

"Don't look at me like that!" Mum laughed. "You'll understand, one day!"

"Sure," I said, unconvinced.

"Can we hurry it up please!" Dad called from downstairs, impatiently.

"I'd better go," I said, giving her a quick hug before hurrying off downstairs. As much as I loved Mum, being in her office with all those different flowers could be overwhelming. I heard Rosie's door slam shut and knew she'd be in a foul mood when we got into the car. If there was one thing you did not do, it was interrupt her beauty regime.

"Hurry up!" came the voice of my youngest brother, Fionn. He was so annoying! Fionn had stared at St Phillip's Secondary in September and was already bringing my near-non-existent coolness level down even more. It didn't help that we looked alike too. We both had Dad's eyes and hair colour, although Fionn kept his hair straight, whereas mine didn't seem to ever do anything beyond curl.

It's not that I didn't like Fionn, I did. Honest! He just... annoyed me. I mean, he liked tests. He asked for homework. He spent most of his evenings camped up in his bedroom actually enjoying reading. Who enjoys reading?

Climbing into Dad's car – a 1957 Chevrolet Bel Air if you're wondering – was like walking into some retro nightmare. He has a thing for classic cars. There were battered old Car and Driver magazines littering the floor, the seats needed reupholstering, and worst of all, Fionn was cramped next to me.

"Why can't I sit in the front?" Fionn whined, sounding more like a toddler than an eleven year old.

"Because Rosie gets car sick," Dad said for the millionth time. "It is easier for her to sit in the front."

Quick fact for you. Rosie does not get car sick. Rosie sits in the front so that she can check her makeup in the mirror.

As we clicked our seatbelts into place, Rosie sauntered into the car. Her hair had been straightened, and she looked – I hate to say it – beautiful.

"Nice of you to join us," said Dad from the driver's seat. His moustache bristling with each word. "Does this mean we are finally ready to go?"

"Yes," I said, setting my bag between my legs and making sure to avoid getting too close to Fionn.

"Good," said Dad, starting the car. "We will pick up Sebastian on the way. Seatbelts!"

Rosie clicked her seatbelt in, taking the time to check her makeup in the mirror (I told you that's why she sits in the front!), and I tried not to think about the last time Seb had climbed into this car. Fionn had spilt Coke all over us, and I had been so angry with him that I was amazed I hadn't burst into flames.

It hadn't helped that Fionn, like most people, was convinced Seb and I were secretly dating. I don't know why they couldn't accept that a boy and a girl could be just friends!

As we pulled up outside Seb's house, I waved at his Mum and Ma, who always came out to see him off.

"I've told them it's embarrassing!" Seb would grumble every day as they waved. I would just laugh and wave right back.

"Hello, Mrs and Mrs Morgan!" Dad called, smiling. There was something about Seb's Mums. You couldn't help but like them.

"Morning Albert!" Dot waved back. "How's the car?"

"Oh no," Seb mumbled, getting in, and shutting the door. "Not the car conversation again."

From the front seat Rosie stifled a laugh. It was a regular thing. At least once a week, Dot and Dad would get into a long winded conversation about Dad's classic Chevrolet, while we all sat around waiting for him to drive the thing.

"Wonderful! Wonderful!" Dad called. "I can't stop, I've got a very busy day!"

Dad worked as a lawyer from some big firm, but he hadn't said anything about being busy today. He was gripping the steering wheel so tightly I was convinced he was going to rip it off.

"Raf's coming," Seb whispered, and I realised why Dad was so eager to get away. I also went as red as Seb's hair.

"Morning Mr S," Raf said, coming to rest against the car.

Raf was Seb's older brother, and was also Rosie's boyfriend. I could see why they liked each other. Raf had long, red hair which he kept tied in a ponytail, and he even managed to make the dull green St Phillip's uniform look good.

26

"Good morning, Rafael. I am afraid the car is full," Dad said stiffly. He had never been fully on board with Rosie and Raf dating, and it didn't look like that was going to change any time soon.

"That's fine, I fancied a walk," Raf said, smiling his most charming smile. "I just wanted to ask Rosie if we were still on for tonight?"

Rosie giggled. I mean, full on, schoolgirl-talking-to-her-crush giggle. How Raf could still make her blush and act like a little kid after they'd been going out for a year baffled me. Beside me, Seb made gagging sounds, and I tried not to laugh. Fionn was too interested in his science homework to pay any attention to what was going on.

"Tonight?" Dad said quickly. "Oh, I don't think she will be available tonight, I am afraid. We have a family tradition you see. Each week we pick a night and turn it into a family film night. Lots of food, drink, that sort of thing."

We most certainly did not have a film night tradition, but it was fun to see Dad panicking.

"Well," said Rosie, putting on her 'I'm going to win this argument' voice, "technically Raf is part of the family now, Dad. So, why not invite him over to share in our tradition?"

She said tradition like it was the most offensive swear word she could think of.

"I... that would... I..."

"Yeah!" I chipped in, earning me a grin from Rosie and Raf. It took me a second to stop focusing on his perfect face and remember what I was saying.

"Yeah, why not invite Seb and his parents as well? That way it's a proper family get together!"

"I'm up for it!" Seb chipped in, grinning at me.

"I suppose... well, very well." Dad finally agreed, looking defeated.

Dot had begun to make her way over, and Dad swallowed.

"Ah, Doro— ow!" Rosie had elbowed him quickly. Nobody, not even Liz, called Dot by her full name.

"Dot," Dad corrected himself, rubbing his side. "We were just saying, it's been a while since you all came over. Why don't you, Liz and the children join us for dinner this evening. We're having a family film night, you see, and Rosie thought it might be nice to invite you all over."

Dot looked at us all in turn, trying to suss out why Dad was inviting her over. We all gave our best 'this-is-perfectly-normal-don't-ask-questions' smiles. She did not seem convinced.

"Why not!" Dot said with a smile.

"Yeah!" Raf grinned, his eyes still on Rosie. "Sounds great Mr S!" Raf smiled. "I'll see you at seven." He smiled at Rosie, who looked like she'd been hit over the head. She leaned forward, evidently hoping for a kiss, but Dad made sure to shut the window before Raf could move any closer.

"Yes, well, goodbye!" Dad called, pulling away from Seb's house and hurtling down the road, mumbling about 'that blasted boy' and 'teenagers'.

St Phillip's Secondary School is in the poshest part of London I've ever seen. It sits opposite a row of perfect houses, all with neat little front gardens and tall trees which give the perfect amount of shade in summer. The school itself is made up of three different buildings, and, according to most of Year 11, used to belong to nuns.

"Ugh," Rosie sighed, as we made our way into the dining hall. It was already full of other students, and Fionn had already left us to join his other Year 7 friends, all of who had their noses

28

in their science books.

"What's wrong?" Seb asked from the other side of Rosie. We were like her own personal bodyguards.

"Jennifer Harris," moaned Rosie. Jennifer Harris was another Year 11, and liked to think she was the Queen Bee of the school. I thought she had too much makeup and too little brain.

Jennifer Harris also had a massive crush on Raf, and had made it her mission in life to cause trouble for him and Rosie since they started dating. She was pale, with blonde hair, and was currently making her way straight towards us.

"Morning Rosie," she said, stopping in front of us. "No Raf today?" she asked, sounding a little too pleased that Raf wasn't with Rosie.

"He's on his way," Rosie said through gritted teeth. "Not that it's any of your business where my boyfriend is."

"I was only asking," Jennifer said, smirking. "It's not my fault if you think he's sneaking off to see someone else."

"Well its lucky I'm here now, isn't it?" said Raf coming up behind Rosie, who looked relieved.

"Raf!" trilled Jennifer, her voice high. "I was just saying—"

"You were just saying," said Raf, his usual smile gone, "that I might be sneaking off to see someone else."

"It was just a joke!" Jennifer said, going red. She'd obviously not expected Raf to overhear her. She barged past us, storming out of the dining hall.

"You shouldn't let her get to you," Raf said, slinging his arm around Rosie.

"I know, I know," Rosie said, sullenly. "She just irritates me, that's all."

"She's just jealous that you've managed to bag the handsomest boy in school." Raf laughed. Seb and I took that as our cue to start walking away, before Raf and Rosie started getting all lovey-dovey in front of us. As we left the dining hall, we saw Levi Carew, a dark-haired boy who we shared most of our classes with looming over a group of Year 7s. Levi was a bully, everyone knew that. He was obviously trying to get them to hand over their lunch money, but just as he was growling about what he would do if they didn't hand it over, Mr Crawford appeared behind him. Mr Crawford was one of our new PE teachers, and had a look that could make even Levi tremble.

"I wasn't doing anything!" he protested. We didn't hang around to hear any more, but we did catch sight of the Year 7s scampering away to their lessons, obviously glad to be out of Levi's line of sight.

We made it out of the dining hall just in time for the bell to ring for our first lesson. Seb and I were in the same class for most of our subjects, and as we made our way up to the third floor, we could hear people whispering about how Raf had shown Jennifer up by arriving announced in the middle of her little wind-up. It felt good to hear it again, even if people were adding their own little touches to the story. By the time we made it to Mrs Pallas' classroom, Raf had apparently arrived as Jennifer was telling Rosie about how she was the one Raf was in love with – which we knew wasn't true – and had swept Rosie up in his arms and carried her away.

People loved to be dramatic at St Phillip's. Me and Seb just laughed it off and took our seats at the back of the class. We'd been on the same table since the start of the year when Mrs Pallas had arrived. She's different to most of the other teachers. She's in her forties, I think, with greying brown hair and wears bright, yellow glasses and an array of colourful suits, today's choice being hot pink. She also drives a bright red motorbike. She walked into the class, her helmet in one hand, a steaming mug of tea in the other.

"Year 8, settle down!" she called in her cool, commanding voice. Something we had all learnt about Mrs Pallas was that she never repeated herself. The class fell silent, and she took her seat at her polished mahogany desk and flipped her laptop open. Seb and I shared our table with our friend Clara, a small, quiet Asian girl with long black hair and brown eyes. Everyone said she was nerdy and didn't talk, but we knew differently. Clara talked, but only to the people she actually wanted to talk to. It made Seb and me feel special in a way, as if we were part of a secret club. The club of people Clara liked.

Then there was Levi, who already looked like he was spoiling for a fight. As well as terrorising Year 7s, Levi enjoyed graffitiing teacher's cars, and storming out of lessons. We'd all seen the rude words he'd scribbled on Mr Collings, our Maths teacher's car, and he'd even tried to let down the wheels on Mrs Pallas' bike, but she'd caught him. He'd gotten a month's worth of detention for that, and had grumbled everyday about how unfair it was. I don't think Levi had ever made it through an entire lesson without being told off. There were rumours even some of the teachers were scared of him. In fact, the only teachers who didn't seem to be scared of him were Mr Crawford and Mrs Pallas.

"Clara!" Seb whispered quickly. "I need to ask you something!"

Clara looked up, careful to keep herself out of Mrs Pallas' eyeline. Cool as she was, Mrs Pallas did not take kindly to people talking without permission in her lessons.

"What?" Clara whispered, her eyes still trained on the board in front of us, her lips barely moving. She'd perfected the art of

31

making it seem like she was silent, even when she was having full blown conversations.

"It's about Greek myths—" Seb said.

"Now, Year 8, for the rest of the term – settle down I said!" Mrs Pallas growled; her eyes suddenly intense. She must have heard Seb whispering to Clara.

"As I was going to say," she said with a pointed look at Seb. She had definitely heard him. "We will be continuing our work on the Greek myths."

Seb looked delighted at that. Everyone knew Clara was a myth expert, she was always telling us about the different myths her Dad had told her about. But I'd never known Seb to be interested in them too.

"Who can tell me," Mrs Pallas said, her grey eyes passing over each of her students in turn, "who the Twelve Olympians are?"

Several hands shot into the air. From the back of the class, Greg Pinder shouted "Zeus!"

"Very good!" Mrs Pallas said, writing the name down on her whiteboard. "Zeus was King of the Gods, and Lord of the Sky. Who else?"

Samantha Parker gave Demeter, Goddess of the Harvest, Luke Croft gave Apollo, God of Archery, (Seb looked a bit freaked out by that. I decided I'd ask him about it later) James Asher gave Hera, Goddess of Marriage and Seb and me gave Dionysus, God of Wine and Aphrodite, Goddess of Love.

"Excellent, excellent!" cried Mrs Pallas. "That's six of the Twelve! Can we name any more?"

There were a few more answers thrown out. Chloe Woodman gave Artemis, Goddess of the Hunt, and Alice Peregrine gave Hermes, Messenger of the Gods.

"Splendid!" Mrs Pallas put in, writing up the new names. "Let me see, we have Zeus, Hera, Hermes, Dionysus, Apollo, Artemis, Aphrodite and Demeter. Eight! Come on, who can think of the remaining four?"

Clara put her hand up. That was odd. Even though Clara, Seb and I would talk to each other all the time, she never put her hand up in class.

"Clara?" Mrs Pallas prompted, smiling at her.

"Um… Hephaestus?" Clara all but whispered, her pale face going redder by the second. By the time Mrs Pallas stopped staring at her, Clara had gone as red as Seb's hair.

"Hephaestus!" Mrs Pallas exclaimed. "The Smith of the Gods! Excellent, excellent!"

Mrs Pallas looked delighted at that. Clara, on the other hand, looked like she wanted to turn invisible.

"That's nine! Only three left!"

"Hades."

It took us all a minute to work out who had spoken. Every face had turned to stare at Levi, who was scowling at the class. His friends – or rather his gang – were the only ones I ever heard call him by his name. Most people called him 'that one' or 'the Year 8 boy who looks like he could rip your head off'.

"Well," Mrs Pallas said, failing to hide the shock in her voice. "It is not often you grace us with an answer, Mr Carew. But, you are correct! Hades, who never actually had a seat on Olympus, is indeed sometimes counted amongst the Olympians."

Levi just tutted and went back to scowling at the desk as if it had insulted him.

"Anyone else?" Mrs Pallas asked, but no hands went up. "Very well," she said, sounding a little disappointed. "The two gods we are missing from our list are Poseidon" – Mrs Pallas seemed to spit the name out, like it was a sour sweet, "God of the Seas, and Athena, Goddess of Wisdom."

Mrs Pallas looked particularly happy when she wrote 'Athena'. "What I want you to do," she said, "is try to order the gods in term of importance to our modern lives. Which gods might we rely on the most? Which might we think are unnecessary now?"

We got on with it, Clara happily writing down the names in about thirty seconds, while Seb and I were unable to decide between Ares, the God of War and Demeter, Goddess of the Harvest.

"Why would the God of War be more important than the goddess who controls the seasons?" I asked, exasperated.

"Because," said Seb "If I'm playing Call of Duty, I'm going to be praying to Ares for help, aren't I? I'm not going to be looking at my screen and wondering if Demeter can make the grass I'm hiding in look a little greener!"

I rolled my eyes and kept Demeter above Ares. The other tables seemed to be having similar conversations, the low hum of noise easily making everyone sound the same.

"Clara," Seb said, going into his bag and pulling out his maths book. "In the Greek myths, how was Olympus destroyed?"

"It never was," Clara said confidently. "There are people who still believe it's around today."

"Are you sure?" Seb asked, flipping open his book. "There's no myth about Olympus being attacked by monsters and one of the gods going missing?"

"Nerds," Levi mumbled, not looking up from the desk, his worksheet empty.

"Bully," Clara mumbled. I'd never heard her say more than a word to Levi. I caught my breath, waiting for the eruption from him, but he didn't even look up.

"Seb, there's no myth about Olympus being destroyed," Clara explained. "There's the myth about the Aloadaes, Otus and Ephialtes, who tried to climb Olympus, but nothing about it actually being destroyed."

"Seb, what are you talking about?" I asked. He'd never really shown much interest in the Greek myths before, but now he was determined to prove there was a myth Clara, who knew the Greek myths better than anyone, didn't know.

"It must have been," he mumbled, but Clara shook her head.

"Seb, I'm telling you, there isn't. Like I said, there are people who still think it exists today. Not the actual mountain, everyone knows that's still here, but the mythical one. Sorry to prove you wrong, but it never happened. Why do you ask anyway?"

"Oh, just curious!" Seb said breezily. "I just thought it might've. You know, Norse mythology has Ragnarök, I wondered if Greek mythology had something similar, that's all."

One thing you should know about Seb is that he is a terrible, terrible liar. He always has been. I still remember when he tried to lie and say that it was Raf who'd tried to drive Liz's car when we were ten. He'd gone bright red and burst into tears as soon as Liz asked him about it. Whatever reason Seb had for asking about Olympus being destroyed, it had nothing to do with Ragnarök. Even Clara didn't look convinced.

"Everything all right at the back?" Mrs Pallas called. We looked up. She was staring at our table with those intense grey eyes, and I was sure she'd heard every word we'd said.

"Fine, Mrs Pallas," I called out. "Just discussing where Ares should go on the list!"

Mrs Pallas nodded, and returned to her laptop, apparently convinced everything was fine.

Between us, Clara and I spent the rest of the lesson sharing looks that clearly meant 'somethings-wrong-with-Seb-he's-being-weirder-than-usual'. He was so sure that there was a myth Clara didn't know about, and everyone knew Clara knew every Greek myth there was. She could recite them on command, if you asked her to. So why was he so sure she didn't know this one?

I looked out of the window and saw Raf in the middle of a PE lesson. He was in the middle of the school's football pitch, tearing through the other team's defenders. Everyone at St Phillip's said Raf had potential to play professionally, and watching him weave his way past the other team and score, I could understand why. Mr Crawford blew his whistle and Raf's team piled on top of him, their cheers reaching up through Mrs Pallas' windows. I was so focused on staring at Raf, I didn't even notice that there was a man outside the classroom door until Levi barked out "Who the hell is that?"

I looked up just in time to see that Mrs Pallas, normally so calm and collected, had gone deathly white and was shaking.

"Miss, are you all right?" I called, but I got no answer. Mrs Pallas was muttering to herself, over and over again. The entire class had gone silent and still. I looked around and saw Greg Pinder, his pen halfway to his worksheet. Luke Croft was holding an elastic band, trying to fire a scrunched up piece of paper at Samantha Parker. It would've looked like a totally normal lesson, if any of them were actually moving. I looked out of the window, and saw that Raf and the rest of his class were frozen in mid-celebration. Only Mr Crawford, his hands deep in his pockets seemed to be moving, rooting around for something.

"What is going on?" Seb asked. By the look of it, the four of us and Mrs Pallas were the only people in the room who weren't frozen in time.

"Mrs Pallas," Clara called, "what's going on?"

We looked at the man outside the door, and he stared back at us. He was old and stooped, and when he smiled at us my insides ran cold.

"Be gone," demanded Mrs Pallas, her voice shaky. "Be gone from this realm, Father Time."

As if he had no choice but to obey, the old man vanished, and the class roared back into life, as if nothing had happened.

But something had happened, I was sure of it, even if the memory of the last few minutes was growing fuzzy in my brain.

"Did you guys—"

"Yeah," said Levi. "I noticed him. The old man at the door."

"Who was he? A governor?" offered Seb.

"Do governors normally make time stop?" Levi scoffed.

"Time couldn't have stopped," Clara said, but she didn't sound sure.

The four of us looked over at Mrs Pallas, who was slumped in her chair. She was typing away on her computer as if nothing had happened, but she was still deathly white. She raised her head and caught our eyes, and in that moment I knew she remembered what happened.

Things had just gotten very, very weird.

Chapter Three
Levi

I wasn't imagining it. There had definitely been an old man stood outside our classroom, and Mrs Pallas had ordered him to leave. But it was more than that. Something else had happened when he'd appeared. I'd been staring at the door, counting down the minutes until the end of the lesson, when I'd have the chance to scare some Year 7s into giving me their lunch money. I'd almost gotten a few of them earlier, but Mr Crawford had interfered. He was always doing that. Every time I tried to approach some of the Year 7s, he'd appear out of nowhere to get on my case.

It's not like I don't deserve it, I know I do. I cause trouble, and what's more, I enjoy it. I know I shouldn't be a bully, we're always having assemblies on why bullying is wrong, and there are posters plastered all over the school that say NO BULLYING in massive capital letters.

I still do it though. And I don't know why. My teachers back in primary school used to say I had some anger problems, but Mum always said they didn't know what they were talking about. Some of them even used to say it was because my Dad wasn't around, but Mum would usually just ignore them. I didn't like scaring Year 7, but I still did it. It made me feel important.

As for the messing around, causing teachers to lose their temper?

I love that! Don't get me wrong, I know it isn't fair on the other kids, but I can't help it. It's like I've been hardwired to enjoy messing around. And I never actually hit anyone when I was in one of my moods. I just shouted and kicked a few walls. There was always a little voice in my head that told me it was wrong to take it out on people, and there must have been a part of me that was listening, like it was trying to make into a better person.

But right now, I was pushing that voice right down so that I could focus on what had happened in our English lesson. I hated English, mainly because I was sat at the back with the three nerdiest people in my year. Seb, Frankie and Clara were the worst people to be sat with in any lesson. For a start, Clara actually enjoys school. Who enjoys school? The only reason I haven't tried to start on Seb more often is because of his brother. Everyone knows Raf wouldn't be afraid to turn the tables on me if I ever started on his brother. I tried it on Frankie's brother once. He's a nerd in the year below, so he should have been an easy target, but I didn't count on Raf seeing the whole thing. He went absolutely beserk, and I've avoided Fionn Sibanda ever since. I just turn my anger onto Frankie every now and then.

And I know, you're probably thinking that I'm the worst person around. But I did have some good qualities. I help out at my mum's little café when I can, and I help look after Gran. But when it comes to school, it's like someone had flipped a switch that makes me go from well-behaved to an utter nightmare, and everyone else has to pay the price.

Our lesson had been another of Mrs Pallas' boring ones on the Greek myths. Mum had brought me a book, back when I was in primary school that was full of the old myths about the gods. I always pretended I never really cared for it, but – and if you tell anyone this, I'll make you regret it – I'd read it about a hundred times. I loved all the stories about the gods, how they were always getting mixed up in human affairs and fighting monsters.

But I never told anyone. I had a reputation to up.

I think that was why Mrs Pallas had looked so shocked when I'd named one of the gods. She'd tried to hide it, but I could see she had expected me to know nothing about them. Well, I did. Shows her what she knows.

I kept it a secret, but I thought my knowledge of the gods might be as good as Clara's. She was a nerd, but she knew her stuff when it came to the myths. She also hardly ever said a word to me, which is why I'd nearly fallen out of my chair when she'd called me a bully. Clara, who never said a word except to Frankie and Seb, had called me a bully. If it had been anyone else, I would've flown off the handle and started kicking things, but there was something about it being Clara that stood up to me, that stopped me dead in my tracks. Clara was... interesting. She barely said a word to anyone, and yet being alone never seemed to bother her. The people who whispered 'nerd' (and much worse) as she walked past them? She didn't even acknowledge them. So why, after ignoring all my attempts at getting to her last year, all the comments, the attempts to trip her up, after all of that had she chosen today to talk back to me?

As if having Clara stand up to me wasn't weird enough, that old man had appeared and frozen time.

No. He hadn't frozen time. It was just one of those moments when everything's going so slow you think time's been frozen. It had to be.

Frankie and Seb had been insistent time had been frozen. They'd tried to catch up with me once we'd left the classroom, but I'd been too quick. I'd run out of there as soon as I could. I barged my way past other students, snarling at them. I wouldn't allow myself to get freaked out by it. I knew what had happened. The man was a governor, or an inspector, or maybe a prospective parent. He was just having a tour of the school, and he stood outside for so long that we all thought time had stopped. That was it. It was the only real explanation. And who knows why Mrs Pallas looked so scared when she saw him. Maybe he was a governor at her old school, or another teacher. Maybe they had history. Everyone always said Mrs Pallas led a secret life with a dodgy past. Maybe he was part of it.

He had not frozen time! He couldn't have.

It had been a few hours since our English lesson. I'd skipped my Maths lesson, and was just debating whether to actually go to double science when an idea came to me. I could go back to Mrs Pallas' classroom. I told myself I wanted to see if I could annoy her enough into giving me a detention. I'd just skip it anyway, and that would annoy her more. Sounded perfect to me. I ignored the small voice in my head that kept saying I was going back to see if the old man was there. For about the hundredth time since our English lesson, I told myself that freezing time was completely impossible, and that it hadn't happened.

When I got back to Mrs Pallas' classroom, after dodging past the other rooms to avoid being spotted skiving off of double science – who needs science? – I expected to find Mrs Pallas sat at her desk, marking some essays, or maybe in the middle of another lesson. Oh, that would be brilliant! I could annoy her, and an entire class!

The door to her classroom was closed, but from where I was stood, I still get a good look inside through the glass window. A voice in my head told me that the window was there so that other members of staff could see inside, not for students to spy on their teachers, but I ignored it. I was going to enjoy winding Mrs Pallas up.

Mrs Pallas was stood by her desk, but not in the same hot

pink suit she'd worn earlier. She was dressed in a sharp grey suit, and her hair was longer. On the desk, where her laptop had been, was now a scale model of what looked like a city, with real smoke rising up from it. As I stared at it, Mr Crawford came into view on the other side of the door. He had his back to me, blocking my view of the model city, and his voice was raised. He was in his usual tracksuit, and I could clearly see the two snake tattoos he had running across his arms.

All the girls say that the tattoos make him look hot, but I think he looks like an idiot. They're a really bright shade of green and look like a three year old has drawn them on his arm. Hardly a masterpiece.

"What you think happened is not the issue here, Athena! The issue is that it happened, and you did not raise the alarm!"

Athena? Everyone knew Mrs Pallas' first name was Erika. She even wore a necklace with it on, and we'd all seen her name when she was locked out of her computer (another pleasure of mine). What's more, Mr Crawford hardly ever raised his voice to his students, so what was he doing shouting at another member of staff?

I know what you're thinking. I shouldn't have eavesdropped, I should have just turned around and walked away like a good student.

News flash – I am not a good student.

"Keep your voice, down Hermes!" Mrs Pallas shot back. "Do you want the entire ruddy school to hear us?"

Hermes? Mr Crawford's first name was Max, so who was this Hermes guy? And what were they shouting about? I edged closer to the door, waiting for them to continue.

"Athena, this is serious. We have managed to conceal ourselves at this school for six months without anyone suspecting a thing. You and I both know how hard Hades worked to establish a link with the mortal boy, how many deals he had to make with Morpheus. It could all be for nothing if Father Time has gone over to their side!"

I was right up against the door now, my head just out of sight of the two adults. There was no chance I was going to miss out on the rest of this argument. Not after hearing that!

So Mrs Pallas and Mr Cranford weren't really teachers! And whoever this Hades guy was, he'd established a link with someone! I ran through all the different possibilities for why they'd be hiding in the school. Athena, Hades and Hermes had to be code names. Spies? Criminals? And who – or what – was the mortal they'd established a link with?

"If the Constellation Council heard so much of a whisper that Father Time was here, that he is walking once more on Earth, they will demand that we give up our lives here. If they suspect, even for a moment, that he is doing the bidding of Erebus, we'll be forced to relinquish our very existence!" barked Mr Cranford savagely.

"I know that!" said Mrs Pallas, sounding frustrated.

"Athena, Father Time was able to infiltrate this school. He got past every piece of protection we put in place. As if that wasn't worrying enough, he was noticed! By four mortal children!" Mr Crawford said.

I heard myself breathe in sharply. I tried, desperately, to push away the memory of what Mrs Pallas – or whatever her was – giving an order to the old man who had been at the door. She had called him Father Time, too.

It really had happened.

"You have made your point!" Mrs Pallas snapped. "Just remember, Hermes, I am not the only one who allowed a job to

43

go wrong! Or have you forgotten about father?"

Mr Crawford let out a low whistle. "Low blow, Athena. Very low blow."

"I'm sorry," Mrs Pallas said. "I should not have said that."

"No, you should not. We shall need to inform the others that Father Time was here. With some luck, we may still be able to convince him to join us in the hunt for Father. We shall leave here together."

Whoever Father Time was, the fact he had been at the school was obviously not a good thing. I tried to get my thoughts into some kind of order. If Mrs Pallas and Mr Crawford really were spies or criminals, then maybe Father Time was a police officer, or another spy. That still didn't explain how he had been able to get into the school though, I told myself.

I didn't have time to dwell on it, because Mr Crawford had opened the door and was storming out.

Uh oh. There was nowhere to hide. He was going to see me, and demand to know how much I'd heard, and then haul me off to some secret location and kill me.

"We regroup tonight, Athena," he said coldly, as if he hadn't noticed me. "We inform Queen Hera and the others of your failure to detect Father Time's presence."

Mr Crawford, or Hermes, or whoever he was, didn't look like Mr Crawford any more. His hair was a bright shade of blonde, his muscles were more pronounced, and strangest of all, he was holding a two metre long staff, which had engravings of snakes all over it.

At least, I thought they were engravings, until one of them winked at me.

"Once the others have been informed, we will decide on a battle plan to retrieve father. If the information we have is correct, he will be back with us in a matter of days, after which he will decide your fate."

Mrs Pallas stormed out after him. Her face was harder, and she looked infinitely more cross than I had ever seen her.

"A battle plan!" she spat incredulously. "We had a battle plan Hermes, and you ruined it! If you had not been so distracted, we would not be in this mess! Summon the others. Summon the Zodiacs, and the Amazons and the Atlanteans! Let them judge me for trying to find Father! They will judge you just as harshly!"

By the time Mrs Pallas had finished, Mr Crawford, or Hermes, or whoever he was, had vanished. And I mean vanished. Literally disappeared.

I was so focused on working out how he'd done it, I hadn't noticed Mrs Pallas, still in this new form, turn to face me.

"I think you have seen quite enough, Levi Carew," she said in that cold voice. Her eyes were locked on mine again.

I ran like my life depended on it.

Chapter Four
Clara

I had not imagined it. I knew what I had seen. A man, dressed entirely in black, with rotten teeth and sunken eyes had been stood outside our English class.

But why had no one else noticed except Seb, Frankie, Levi and me? He wasn't a teacher or a governor, and he looked far too old to be a parent. And what had he done to make it feel like time had stopped?

Levi had disappeared as quickly as he could once English finished, so I hadn't had the chance to talk to him about it. He was probably already on the hunt for another Year 7 to steal money from.

"There was no one there!" Chloe had said when I mentioned what had happened during Maths. She had been the sixth person to tell me that, but I knew I'd seen someone. And I was certain Mrs Pallas had seen him too. When we looked over at her desk, she had looked terrified. I was certain that this man was the reason. She had seen the same man I had. And she had called him something. I shook my head, trying to force the memory to come back to me. It felt as though it was fading right out of my head. Mrs Pallas had definitely called him something!

It was like he'd appeared out of nowhere, right in front of the door. One second the corridor had been empty, the next, he'd been looming against the doorframe, his eyes on Mrs Pallas.

I don't know why I was so determined to find out what had happened. There was a voice in my head that kept saying 'leave it', but I ignored it. If there really was a stranger in school, and he really could make time stop, someone had to do something.

That was why I found myself sneaking back to the English corridor when I should have been in double science. I'd concocted the perfect plan for finding out what Mrs Pallas knew about the stranger. I'd already lied to Mrs Dellacott, my science teacher, and told her I had an urgent meeting with Mrs Pallas to discuss my grades and had forged a handwritten note from Mrs Pallas explaining why I was out of class in case I got stopped by anyone.

I wasn't as much of a goody-two-shoes as people thought I was. I'd perfected the art of forging notes by teachers within my first week in Year 7, and I was no stranger to telling some white lies. All I had to do was make it to Mrs Pallas' classroom and find out what she knew about our time-stopping intruder. It would be easy.

I hoped.

I heard the shouting before I got near the classroom. It sounded like Mrs Pallas was really laying into someone, and that never happened. I hung back, pressing myself against the wall, hoping I was almost invisible. I looked around. Every other classroom door was closed, and there was an eerie silence that didn't feel natural. What's more, I saw Levi with his head against the door, no doubt up to something. The last thing I needed was him seeing me here.

Looking back, I should have just turned around and left. It was all nonsense, the thought that someone was hiding in the school. After all, everyone knew it was impossible to get out of St Phillips's without permission, and it had to be the same for getting in without permission, didn't it?

"What you think happened is not the issue here, Athena!"

47

The sudden bark of voice made me jump. It was the voice of Mr Crawford, one of our PE teachers.

What was he doing, rowing with Mrs Pallas? As far as I knew, they hardly had anything to do with one another. Despite all my senses telling me to run, I edged a little further along the wall, making sure I kept out of Levi's line of sight. The last thing I needed was for him to see me and tell everyone I was sneaking out of lessons.

If I'd been paying attention to what was happening around me, I might have noticed that the voices from Mrs Pallas' classroom had faded away. I might even have seen the man appear.

It was the same man as before. Same sunken eyes, same tattered black clothes, same rotten teeth. His mouth was twisted into the most terrifying smile I'd ever seen.

"Good afternoon." He smiled, showing off those rotting, black teeth. "I have been trying to find you, Clara."

I tried to run, but I couldn't move. My feet wouldn't obey, and I found myself stood face to face with him.

"A necessary precaution," he said, still smiling that twisted smile. "You will be able to move quite freely once our conversation is over."

I tried to call out, to do anything to get Levi's attention. Surely he could see this man in front of me?

"I'm afraid we are quite invisible to your classmate," he said. "A minor advantage for beings like me, you see. I can manipulate time itself. When I release you – if I release you – no time at all will have passed for your classmate. He will continue to spy on your teachers as if nothing has happened."

"Let me go!" I shouted, trying in vain to move.

"It will be easier on us both if you do not struggle," the man said. "It can be so exhausting, watching you mortals tire yourselves out. No wonder the Primordials do not enjoy it."

"Primordials?" I repeated. Nothing he was saying was making any sense.

"Yes. The First Beings, if you like. The beings made up of thought and consciousness alone."

"Like in the Greek myths?" I said, trying to keep the panic out of my voice.

"Exactly," said the man, his face still twisted into that terrifying smile. "You know an awful lot about the myths, don't you, Clara?" he asked, sounding strangely impressed.

"No," I lied, hoping it'd make him leave me alone.

"Oh, Clara," he said, disappointed. "It would be much easier for us both if you told the truth."

He took a step towards me, and before I could react, I could feel him inside my head. He was walking through my memories as if they were a shop, stopping to look at the most interesting moments of my life. I saw Baba and Mama at my tenth birthday, my first day at St Phillip's, my first meeting with Seb and Frankie. Every moment that made me Clara seemed to flash before me, as he walked through my mind.

"How interesting!" he said, smiling that horrible smile again. "Such a lonely girl... no siblings. Hardly any friends... so desperate to do well..."

"Get out of my head!" I screamed, trying to shove at him, but without success.

"Aha!" he shouted in triumphant. "Just what I wanted!"

I don't know if he was triggering my memories, but I suddenly thought of all the books Baba had brought me. Books on every kind of mythology you could think of. Greek, Norse, Celtic, Arthurian, Chinese, Indian.

Books I had read over and over until I was a walking, talking myth expert. Baba had read them to me, time and time again when I was little. I was always asking him what had happened to the gods and heroes, and he would always smile and pull down one of the books from my bookcase and start at the beginning again.

"You know your myths," the man trawled. "Your knowledge will be useful to Erebus."

"Who?" I managed to say, long forgotten memories still swarming my mind.

"Erebus," repeated the man who was invading my mind. "The Primordial Deity of Darkness. The King of Olympus, and Lord of all creation. He has been waiting for you for a long time."

"Waiting for me?" I repeated. None of this made any sense!

"Correct," said the man. "You are going to become his servant, Clara Liu, as has been foretold."

Without warning, the man stepped back from me, and left my memories. I stumbled on the spot, trying to keep my balance.

"Foretold by who?" I demanded, my head swimming.

"By Pythia herself," said the man simply. "The prophecy was simple. It spoke of a girl who would be found in this dump," he said dismissively, taking in the corridor around him. The paint on the walls was starting to crack a little, and the NO BULLYING posters were frayed and faded. "A girl who had supreme knowledge of our history and will be instrumental in ensuring the Sky God is kept hidden away."

"None of this makes any sense!" I pleaded. "Why can't you leave me alone?"

"Because," said the man coldly. "It was foretold. I have been watching you for a long time, Clara Liu, and when I present you to Lord Erebus, I shall be rewarded!"

50

Memories suddenly burst into my head. I had seen this man before! He had hidden himself near my old primary school! He had been outside my house watching me grow up! Every time I had gone to tell Mama or Baba, he had vanished, along with the memory of him!

"You've been spying on me!" I cried out.

He nodded, looking pleased with himself. "I hid myself in plain sight! For thirteen years, I have waited in the shadows, waiting for the perfect moment to deliver you to Lord Erebus! And now, just when those foolish gods think they have a chance of finding their leader, I shall present you to Lord Erebus! He shall ensure Zeus is kept hidden away, and I shall claim my reward!"

"I won't help you!" I said defiantly. "I won't!"

"Foolish mortal," the man said, grinning. "Do you think you have any choice?"

"Who are you?" I demanded, trying in vain to back away from him.

"My name is lost to legend," he said, in his cold high voice. "But you will know me as Father Time. You will serve Lord Erebus well, Clara," Father Time said, grinning. He raised his eyes to the ceiling and said in a loud, clear voice, "She has been found, my Lord! Send your brave solider to take her! Make her your instrument of destruction, Lord Erebus! She is found!"

I let out a scream as the ceiling above me cracked and ripped itself open. From high above, a figure descended down. He was dressed entirely in black, with a tight-fitting black jacket and trousers, and his long black hair flowed past his shoulder. His eyes were completely black, as if someone had coloured every last part of them in with felt tip.

"IS IT SHE?" he said. His voice sent a chill down my spine.

It sounded like every nightmare I had ever had.

"It is," said Father Time. "I have walked through her mind. She has knowledge and power. She is the one Pythia foretold us of."

"YOU HAVE DONE WELL, FATHER TIME," said this new man. "ONCE THE GODS ARE CRUSHED, OUR LORD WILL REWARD YOU. FOR NOW, TAKE UP YOR DAILY TASK. WALK AMONGST THE MORTALS. REPORT WHAT YOU HEAR OF YOUR MISSING SON," he said, a hint of mockery in his voice.

"He is no son of mine!" croaked Father Time. "No son at all! He is a disgrace! He deposed his own father from his throne!"

"AFTER YOU HAD SWALLOWED HIM AND HIS SIBLINGS WHOLE," the new man laughed. "HARDLY BLAMELESS, WERE YOU?"

"Do not mock me!" shouted Father Time. "I am King of the Titans!"

"YOU WERE KING OF THE TITANS," the other man said. "NOW YOU ARE NOTHING BUT A PEST. BE GONE, BEFORE I TURN MY POWERS ON YOU INSTEAD OF THIS GIRL."

"Cronus!" I breathed out, finally realising who he was. "You're Cronus!"

"Correct," said the old man. "I was leader of the Titans. Overthrown by my vicious, ungrateful son and cursed to walk forever on this plain, counting every second of eternity. But Lord Erebus, wise, generous, Lord Erebus, he has new plans for me, oh yes! When you have assisted him in his great plan, I shall be rewarded!"

"ENOUGH!" snapped the other man. "IT IS TIME THIS YOUNG LADY DISCOVERED HER PURPOSE, DO YOU

NOT THINK, CRONUS?"

The Titan laughed, a cold, wheezy laugh. "I do, I do!" he cackled.

"YOU WILL BE OF GREAT SERVICE, CLARA LIU," smiled the other man.

"Who are you?" I asked, trying again to move, but still finding myself stuck to the floor.

"HOW RUDE OF ME," said the man, with a sick smile. "ALLOW ME TO INTRODUCE MYSELF. I AM THANATOS, THE PRIMORDIAL DEITY OF DEATH. AND YOU, CLARA LIU, ARE GOING TO HELP ME DESTROY THE GODS."

I tried to scream, to run, to do anything to get me away from him, but Cronus had made sure I couldn't move. I could only watch as Thanatos stepped forward and placed his hand on my forehead. The next thing I knew, everything went black.

I didn't know who I was any more.

All I knew was I had one purpose.

DESTROY THE GODS.

Chapter Five
Levi

I ran until I was clear of the school. It was easy to get out without being noticed, if you knew how. The school gates were only able to be opened by the reception desk, but if you were skinny enough, you could squeeze through a gap between the gate and the wall. I'd started needing to breathe in, but I could still make it out without too much trouble. Everyone knew the security cameras that the school had installed were just there for show. I'd made it out without being seen and had carried on running, finally winding up in Regent's Park. It was my go-to place when I needed to get away from school. The park was big enough that I could find a tree and sit under it without anyone really stopping to stare at me, and if anyone from the school should come looking, I could always climb up it until I was out of sight.

I slid down into the shade of the biggest tree I could find, sitting on my jumper instead of the damp grass. Today had been a lot to take in. Whoever Mrs Pallas really was, she wasn't a teacher. Teachers did not go about talking in code and wearing battle armour. I'd never really paid attention to Mrs Pallas before. I mean, I tried to, but I found her lessons so boring. We were always reading the same books, over and over. By the time we'd finished our first term with her, I could quote A Christmas Carol back to front if you asked me to. It wasn't that I didn't like English, or reading. I just struggled with it. There were times I wished I could be like Clara, always with my nose in a book, but it didn't happen for me. I'd never found a book that I actually liked. Everyone else in my class thought Mrs Pallas was the best teacher we'd ever had. Well, I would show them! I began to form a plan in my head. I would go back to the school, and would tell her what I'd seen. She wouldn't want people to know she was a criminal or a spy, and I bet she'd do anything to keep it secret. I could make her give me A's on my tests if I promised to keep it secret.

There was a voice in my head that was telling me it was wrong, that it was blackmail. But I didn't listen. I could even try and get money from her!

Yeah, I could demand money in exchange for keeping things quiet! She'd have to agree, otherwise I'd go straight to Mr Fenner, our Headmaster and tell him Mrs Pallas wasn't really a teacher! And if Mr Crawford wasn't a teacher either, I could get double the money!

From somewhere deep in my school bag, my phone began to ring. I rummaged around in my bag, and pulled it out. It was old and the screen was cracked, but it still worked. My screensaver had been the same since Mum had brought me the phone last year. It was an old photo of Mum, me, Nan and Granddad from when I was a little kid. We were sat around Nan and Granddad's dining table at Christmas, and were all wearing those stupid hats you get in crackers. I didn't know it then, but that was the last Christmas we spent with Granddad. He'd died the following summer, and Nan had moved in with us a few months later. She'd sold their big house up in Scotland. She said it was 'full of too many memories' and she couldn't stay there, so now, she stayed with us. The flat we shared was a little small for three people, but it was nice.

'MUM CALLING' my phone flashed up. I sent it to voicemail. I guessed the school had realised I'd done a bunk and had phoned Mum.

"Where are you?" Mum said, when I listened to the voicemail. "Levi, you have got to stop doing this! The school have said, if you don't pull your socks up and start taking your education seriously they're going to kick you out! I cannot believe, after every conversation we've had—"

I clicked the phone off and tossed it back into my bag where it connected with some of my textbooks. All Mum seemed to do lately was moan at me about school. That, or spend all her time at the café. I slid further back against the tree, and looked around the park. There was the usual crowd of mums with prams and joggers trying to look like they weren't out of breath.

That's when the woman caught my eye.

She was, what, forty? Fifty? She had long blonde hair, and was carrying an empty box, the kind that delivery drivers would use when they were dropping off the latest food for Mum's café. She was kneeling down, pulling flowers up from the ground and muttering to herself.

"Rosa canina," she said, just loud enough for me to hear. "Growing nicely."

She had pulled up a few pale pink roses, and was putting them in her box. She'd moved a few steps to the left, and was focusing on a group of purple and green flowers. She dropped them into the box as if it burned her hands to touch them.

"Atropa belladonna," she was muttering. "Dangerous, dangerous flowers. I must speak to the others about this."

I don't know what I found so fascinating about this flower-picker. She looked like any other middle-aged woman I'd seen in the park before, but I couldn't stop staring at her. She was still going, picking up different flowers and chucking them into her box as if she did this every day. She was so absorbed in her picking that she didn't notice the police officer walking up behind her until he tapped her on the shoulder.

"Can I help you?" she asked, still trying to pick a particularly stubborn flower.

"What do you think you are doing?" the officer asked, taking in the box that was quickly filling up with flowers.

"What does it look like I'm doing?" said the woman, finally pulling the flower out and dropping it into the box. "I'm picking flowers for my shop, if you must know."

"Madam," said the officer. He was starting to sound irritated with her now. I watched the two of them, hoping I was about to see an argument unfold. I always loved watching people who weren't me get into trouble. It made for a nice change. "You are not permitted to pick flowers from one of the Royal Parks."

"Oh, nonsense," said the woman. She was still moving along the flower patches, picking and choosing which flowers she wanted to add to her box.

"If you do not stop, I shall be forced to arrest you!" said the police officer through gritted teeth.

"For picking flowers?" laughed the woman. "Don't talk rubbish."

The police officer had obviously had enough. He reached into his belt and pulled out his handcuffs, but just as he was getting ready to arrest the woman, she turned around to face him, and when she spoke her voice was low and powerful.

"You are going to turn around," she said slowly. "You are going to walk away. You will forget you have ever seen me. You will not approach this flowerbed again. You will carry on with your daily duties with no memory of me, or of our meeting."

The officer, his face blank, began to walk away. The woman returned to the flowerbeds as if nothing had happened.

"Ah!" she said happily. "Epigogium aphyllum! I haven't seen these for years!" she said, as she pulled a small, pale flower from its place in the bed and dropped it into the box. The police officer was already out of sight.

What had she done to make him go away? She'd told him to forget that he had ever seen her, but that was impossible.

Unless, said my brain, *she's the same as Mrs Pallas!*

No. I pushed the thought out of my head. Mrs Pallas was a criminal. This woman – whoever she was – had somehow been able to make a police officer forget that he had been about to arrest her. Criminals couldn't do that.

Witches can my brain said. I almost laughed out loud. Even if witches were real – which they're not, I told my brain – everyone knew witches were old women who spent all their time either flying on broomsticks with black cats or stooped over cauldrons, making potions.

That's why the flowers are for! whispered my brain.

I caught her eye as she walked past me, her box overflowing with different coloured flowers. She smiled at me and walked away, back towards the exit.

I got up and grabbed my bag. I didn't know why I was following her, but I was. I kept back just far enough so that if she turned around she wouldn't be able to make out my face, but close enough that I could follow where she was going. She walked quickly, almost like she knew someone was following her. She ducked into side-streets and into large crowds, but I kept as close as I could. Eventually, she came to stop outside a large florists. The windows were packed full of displays, vibrant coloured flowers fighting each other to be seen. The sign above the door was faded, but I could make out the name THOMPSON PALMER. There was what looked like a real rose hanging from the N of Thompson, complete with bright red petals that came down to the tip of the doorway. The woman hurried in, careful not to spill any of her flowers from the box. I waited a few minutes, keeping just out of sight of the doorway. I still couldn't explain why I was following her. I told myself it was because of what she had done to the policeman, but there was something else. I had a feeling in my stomach, like I needed to follow her. Like, somehow, we were connected.

But we couldn't be. I'd never seen her before in my life, and yet here I was, getting ready to go into her shop.

I took a deep breath and walked in.

The inside of the shop was huge. It had looked like any other shop from the outside, but the inside looked like someone had multiplied the outside by about one hundred. The walls seemed to go on and on with no end, and every inch of them was covered in flowers. The whole shop smelt like every kind of flower you could imagine, along with – what was it? – something else, something like fresh fruit. I pushed my way past buckets full of bright roses, avoiding the low hanging leaves of tropical plants. At the far end of the shop there was a small tree that had been planted into a jet black pot, with reddish-purple fruit hanging low from its branches.

"Hello?" I called out, my voice echoing through the shop.

The woman I had been following emerged from—

I blinked, then blinked again. I had to be seeing things. She had walked straight out of the plant, which had opened up to reveal an elegant staircase of marble, leading down...

I shook my head. The plant hadn't opened up, that was ridiculous. The woman had obviously come up from the staircase that led down to the basement of the shop. The plant just looked like it had opened up to let her out because of how close it was to the stairs, that was all.

Then why, my brain countered, *did the plant just close?*

I looked at it, and knew my brain was right. Yes, I might have been arguing with my brain, which was pretty odd, but I wasn't seeing things. The plant had closed up as the woman stepped out of it, and the marble staircase had vanished along with it.

"Oh dear," said the woman quickly. "I mean, hello. Welcome to my shop. I'm Nicki. I'm human. Who are you?"

I ran through what she had just said. So, it was her shop. Her name was Nicki. She was human… who says that?

"I'm Levi," I said. "Levi Carew."

"Hello Levi," said Nicki. "What are you doing in my shop?"

"Um…" I had to think of a convincing lie. "Um… I wanted to buy some flowers for my mum."

It wasn't a complete lie. I had some money in my bag, and Mum always said our flat could do with some flowers to brighten it up.

"How lovely!" Nicki said. She sounded a bit more relaxed, but when she came towards me, I could sense she was still nervous. "Did you have any specific flowers in mind?" she asked.

"Those ones look nice," I said, pointing towards a bouquet of bright white flowers.

"Chrysanthemums!" Nicki said, picking them up. "A wonderful choice! Did you know a white chrysanthemum symbolises loyalty and devoted love?"

While Nicki was telling what all the different coloured blossoms on chrysanthemums symbolise, I had taken the opportunity to approach the tree at the back of the shop. The fruits on it seemed to pulse, and there was a low hum coming from its branches.

I reached out to touch one of the fruits, my hands almost around it—

"DO NOT TOUCH THAT!"

Nicki had flown across the room, and pulled me back from the tree. Her face had turned red with anger, and her voice had gone as low and powerful as when she had made the police officer forget about her.

"Who are you?" she demanded, her eyes trained on me.

"I told you," I said moodily. "Levi Carew. I saw you in the park."

"Damn!" Nicki said hotly. "How much did you see?"

"You were picking flowers," I said. "And then you made the policeman who stopped you forget he'd even seen you."

She didn't even try to deny it. Her shoulders slumped, and when she spoke again, her voice was quiet.

"Was it only you who saw?"

"I think so," I said, confused. "At least, I wasn't with anyone."

"That's good," said Nicki. "I can contain one mortal."

I thought back to what I'd overheard at school. Mrs Pallas and Mr Crawford had used the word mortal.

"You're a criminal," I said, my brain working overtime to link everything together. "You must have sprayed the police officer with some sort of memory-altering gas! Is that what Mrs Pallas is planning to do to all of us at school?" I asked before I could stop myself.

"Mrs Pallas?" Nicki repeated slowly. "Erika Pallas?"

"I didn't say anything about Mrs Pallas," I said stupidly. Nicki raised her eyebrows.

"What do you know about Erika?" she asked.

"I know she's a criminal," I said, trying to work out how I could get out of the shop and run home. "And I'm not the only one who knows! Seb and Frankie saw her too!" I shouted.

Big mistake.

"Erika is not a criminal, Levi. And neither is Max

61

Crawford," Nicki said. "Tell me, who are Seb and Frankie?"

"No one," I said. Even if I wasn't friends with them, I couldn't be sure Nicki wasn't a secret axe murderer who was going to hunt them down if I told her who they were. "And if Mrs Pallas and Mr Crawford aren't criminals, then what are they?" I asked, edging slowly away from Nicki and towards the door.

"They are like me. We are family."

I turned and tried to run, but the door slammed shut and locked.

"Let me out!" I shouted. "You can't keep me here!"

"I am afraid," Nicki said, "that you have heard rather too much, Levi Carew. I cannot let you leave. You will remain here for now, while I set out to find whoever Seb and Frankie are."

"Don't hurt them!" I said, still trying to force the door open.

"Hurt them? Why would I want to hurt them? No, I will just… hm, shall we say moderate what they remember of today's events, that is all. Ah-ha!"

Nicki had pulled down some pale red flowers and had plucked a few of them and was tying them into an elegant bouquet. "I shall have to consult with Hestia… that will require skill… still, it is a necessity," Nicki was saying. "You," she indicated me, "will have to remain here."

As she made her way to the door, the flower pots nearest to me burst apart and thick vines caked in dirt wound their way around me and kept me in place.

"My apologies for the vines, Levi," Nicki said as she opened the door, "but I cannot take any chances right now. Farewell."

She waved her hand as she left the shop, and I was sent backwards through the wall until I crashed, tied up in vines, into a pile of boxes. I heard the door lock shut behind Nicki, and realised I was hopelessly, inescapably, trapped.

Chapter Six
Seb

I left school feeling like I'd sat twenty different exams in one go. By the time Ma pulled up to collect us and drive us home, my head was swarming with different images from my dream. There was Apollo firing his arrows, the man who had been covered in shadows, the Alodaes – I'd looked them up after Clara had mentioned them and discovered that they were the two giants who had passed me singing their football chant. On top of that, there had been the whole incident with Mrs Pallas and Father Time, whoever he was. The memory of our English lesson was starting to fade, like someone was trying to pull it out of my head, but bits and pieces still clung on. I remembered Mrs Pallas ordering him to leave, and the strange feeling that time had been frozen, but beyond that, there was nothing. The whole day had just been weird.

Even dinner with the Sibandas couldn't take my mind off of what had happened. Mr Sibanda had ordered pizzas and selected the latest Tom Cruise film for the film. I'd been sat on one of the large sofas in the living room, with Frankie on one side and Mrs Sibanda on the other. Mum and Ma were on the other sofa, talking animatedly with Mr Sibanda about a car he wanted to buy. There were times I thought that all they could talk about was cars.

"I'm telling you," Ma was saying, "go for the Bristol!"

"But it is so expensive!" Mrs Sibanda complained, before Mr Sibanda could answer.

"But we have the money!" Mr Sibanda reasoned through

mouthfuls of pizza. "Why not, Rionach?"

"Because you already own two cars! We don't need a third!" Mrs Sibanda argued back.

I tried to focus on the debate, I really did. I tried staring at a spot on the wall, counting to ten, but nothing worked. Every time I would try to zone in on what model of car the adults were now arguing about, my brain would be overrun by images of Olympus in flames. I had to figure out what that dream had been about! I had been so certain Clara would put my mind at rest, but she'd been adamant there was no myth about Olympus being destroyed.

So why had I dreamed about it?

"Earth to Seb!" Frankie hissed in my ear, making me jump.

"Huh?" I said, coming back to myself. Frankie was pointing towards the back door, which led into the Sibanda's garden.

No one seemed to notice Raf and Rosie sneaking off, their hands clamped together.

"Gross," Frankie snorted. "What does he see in her?"

"I dunno," I said quickly. I had learnt a long time ago to let Frankie have her rants about Rosie, and definitely not to point out that Rosie was the most beautiful girl in school. I zoned out again as Frankie started listing all of Rosie's faults (she took ages in the bathroom, she left her clothes all over the place, she controlled the TV...)

"Kim drives a similar one, but much newer," Mum was saying, no doubt filling Mr Sibanda in on my older sister's car. Kim was off studying at university, and her going away present from my parents had been a retro Toyota Starlet. What they all found so interesting about old cars, I would never understand.

"What's wrong?" Frankie whispered in my ear, after yet another spell of silence from me. It was only now I realised she'd finished her rant about Rosie and had been waiting for me to respond.

"Nothing," I said quickly.

"Liar," Frankie shot back. I should've known it would be impossible to fool her. After thirteen years of friendship, there wasn't much I could lie about to her. She'd heard it all before.

"Something happened last night," I whispered, making sure only Frankie could hear. "I had a really weird dream."

"Do I want to hear this?" she asked.

"Not like that!" I blushed. "I was in this hall, but it was under attack."

"Had you been playing Call of Duty?" Frankie asked sarcastically. I shot her a withering look. "Sorry," she said. "Carry on."

"It was under attack by all these different monsters. Cyclopes, and flying women and a massive buffalo."

"A massive buffalo?" Frankie cut in. "What would a massive buffalo be doing attacking a hall?"

"I don't know!" I said sulkily. "But there was more. This guy appeared, right, and he started shooting at them all with these arrows. I know it sounds mad, but I'm sure he was Apollo, you know, the Greek god, and he looked exactly like Harry Jones—"

"The lead singer of The Boy and His Muses?" Frankie asked. "He is so dreamy."

"But he couldn't have been, could he?" I said, ignoring how she'd gone all doe-eyed thinking about Harry Jones. "I mean, there's no way he could secretly be a Greek god, is there?"

Frankie just looked confused.

"Seb, why are you telling me this?" she asked. I sighed.

"You have to promise not to laugh, or think I'm mad," I said, deadly serious.

"Okay… I promise," said Frankie, sounding worried.

"Frankie, I think it wasn't a dream," I said.

"What else could it have been?" Frankie asked, filling me with relief. She didn't think I was mad!

"I think it was real," I said. "It felt so real, like I was right there. And Apollo looking like Harry, it has to mean something, doesn't it?"

Even as I said it, I knew it sounded insane. But I couldn't shake the feeling I was right.

"Let me get this straight," Frankie said slowly. "You think that Apollo, the Greek god of poetry, is Harry Jones?"

"I know it sounds mad," I countered. "But I know I'm right! That's why I was asking Clara all those questions in English!"

"I knew it!" she whispered back. "I knew there was something going on!"

"You mean you believe me!" I said, astonished.

"Maybe," Frankie said. "At least, I don't think you're mad. Or lying."

I felt so relieved I could've cried. Frankie believed me!

"So what do we do? We can't very well storm up to a famous singer and say 'excuse me, are you Apollo?'" I said.

"We… write to him instead?" Frankie offered.

I didn't have a chance to think of an answer, before the door rang.

"I'll get it!" Mrs Sibanda called, getting up and making her way to the door.

I barely looked up as the new arrival walked into the living room. She was a short woman, maybe a few years older than Mum, with blonde hair. She was holding a large bouquet of flowers, and wore a jacket that had the words 'Thompson-Palmer Florists' printed on the back in blue letters.

66

"Everyone," said Mrs Sibanda, "this is Nicki Thompson-Palmer. My business partner."

Nicki smiled at us each in turn.

"So, this is the famous Nicki," Mr Sibanda smiled. "Rionach has told me so much about you."

Nicki smiled at him, setting the bouquet down on the sideboard and taking Mr Sibanda's chair as he got up.

"Remind me," he called, making his way into the kitchen and returning with another wine glass, "how long have you and Rionach known each other? She's never told me!" he chuckled, pouring out some red wine and offering the glass to Nicki, who took a large swig out of it.

When she lowered the glass, she looked… uncomfortable.

"Well, it's been so long, I can hardly remember myself," she said. "It must have been university. Yes, that's it. We met at University. We were on the same course, weren't we, Rionach?"

"I don't—" Mrs Sibanda began, but Nicki waved her hand. At once, Mrs Sibanda's face settled into a warm smile. "Yes, you're right. We were on the same course."

There was something about how Mrs Sibanda said that that made her sound like a robot. It was like she was completely unaware of the words she was saying. As if that wasn't weird enough, there was something about Nicki that seemed really familiar…

The rest of the night passed by with a mixture of more conversations about cars, Raf and Rosie constantly sneaking off for kisses, and Frankie and me debating where we had seen Nicki before. She wasn't a neighbour, or a teacher, or even a woman we'd passed on the street.

"Maybe she's just got one of those faces?" Frankie suggested. "You know, where you think you've seen them before, but you really haven't."

I didn't buy it. I knew I recognised Nicki from somewhere, but where?

I looked over at her. She seemed ordinary enough. She was happily chatting away to Mrs Sibanda about their time at university, but every now and then she would wave her hand about and Mrs Sibanda's speech would become slow and her head would nod, as if she was trying to keep herself awake.

"Yes," she was saying, "we went to Oxford together. That's why I told Dot and Liz to send Kim there."

Wait... Kim wasn't at Oxford. Kim had never even applied to go to Oxford. So why did Mrs Sibanda think she was there now?

I thought back to last year, when Kim had been applying for universities. She'd spent most her time trying to work out which would be the best one for studying History. She'd even come over to ask the Sibandas for advice.

"It's no good asking me, darling," Mrs Sibanda had said from her office. Frankie and I always said she never knew how loud she was when she was in there. "I didn't go to university. I finished my A-Levels and went straight into working at the shop!"

The memory had hit me like a ton of bricks. We'd all heard the story about how Mrs Sibanda had left school and started working in a small bookshop, only to end up taking it over a few years later.

"Oh, what lovely flowers!" Ma was saying, inspecting bouquet Nicki had brought with her.

"Thank you," smiled Nicki. "I grew them myself. They're a rare species, gladiolus alatus. Apparently, they're wonderful flowers for stimulating the memory."

"Frankie!" I whispered, glad that the adults had started discussing the magical memory flowers Nicki had brought, "Your Mum didn't go to university, did she?"

"No," Frankie whispered back. "She left school and started working in the bookshop. She's told us the story about a million times."

I looked at Nicki. She was chatting away, but she seemed nervous, as if she was expecting that she'd have to run off at a moment's notice. Her eyes wouldn't stay on any of the adults as they talked.

"If your Mum never went to university," I whispered, my eyes on Nicki, "then how did she meet Nicki there?"

"She…" Frankie began. "She can't have…"

"Well, I really should be going," Nicki said, standing up quickly. "It's been lovely to meet you all!"

She was up and out of the door in seconds. She'd been so quick to leave, she'd forgotten her jacket. As I picked it up, I noticed that the letters were faded and peeling, so that instead of reading THOMPSON-PALMER FLORISTS, it actually read THO S N – P L E R FLO ST.

"We'll take it," I said, hauling Frankie to her feet.

"Yeah, she can't have gone far," Frankie agreed as we made our way to the door.

As we grabbed our own coats and headed out, Frankie whispered "Is it just me, or was there something really weird about Nicki?"

"It wasn't just you," I said. "And how come she was able to convince everyone she met your mum at university if your mum never went to university?"

Looking back, I should have realised it was the flowers. After all, Nicki had told us herself that they were good for the memory. If we'd paid attention, things might have turned out differently for us.

But, as we were going to find out, paying attention to what people – especially people like Nicki – told us, was not our strong point.

Chapter Seven
Clara

I don't know how long it had been since Thanatos had invaded my head, but when I looked out of my window the sun was setting. I don't even remember if I'd stayed in school. The last thing I remembered was Thanatos, with that sick smile, walking towards me.

I was home. I was in my bedroom, my bookcases still overflowing with all the books Baba and Mama had brought me. Some of them had bookmarks sticking out of them, some had pages falling out where I'd read them so many times. Some of them were in Chinese, which Baba had been teaching me. He'd always wanted me to learn, and I'd finally agreed last year. So far, I'd mastered the basics, but that was it. It wasn't like I wasn't trying to learn, I just couldn't take it in.

"But why," Mama had said after Baba had spent another hour trying to teach me, "does she have to learn? All of our family lives here, and they all speak English!"

"Because Lian," Baba explained, "it is her heritage! You and I speak it, so Clara should learn it too!"

Mama knew better than to keep pressing Baba about it. If he wanted me to learn, he was going to make sure I learned. He didn't push me, or try to force me to learn, he would just remind me it was my heritage.

I think he just liked teaching me. That was Baba's job. He was a university lecturer who specialised in the study of mythology. That probably explained why he'd filled my bookshelves with all the different mythology books he could find. Mama was a chef for a top London restaurant, and her food was incredible. Whenever Baba or Mama had friends over, they would always ask for second and third helpings of Mama's food. I could smell it now, the familiar waft of spices and the off-key singing Baba would insist on doing whenever Mama was in the kitchen.

"Jonathan," Mama was saying, her voice carrying up the stairs to my bedroom, "you know you can't sing, don't you?"

"How dare you!" Baba laughed. "I have a beautiful voice!"

I wanted to agree with Baba, but he really, really couldn't sing. Even if he did insist on trying every day.

"ENOUGH OF THIS," Thanatos growled in my head as I sat on my bed, listening to Baba trying to sing his way through an old Sinatra song. "IT WILL SOON BE TIME TO VISIT THE HARVEST GODESS. YOU MUST PREPARE YOURSELF. SHE WILL FIGHT BACK, BUT WE MUST PREVAIL. ONCE SHE IS TAKEN, WE CAN MOVE TOWARDS THE OTHERS, AND ONCE WE HAVE SEALED THEM ALL AWAY, LORD EREBUS WILL REWARD ME. USE THE POWERS I HAVE GRANTED YOU, CHILD. SUMMON YOUR BOOKS."

I did as Thanatos commanded and held out my head. From my bookcase, a book sailed and landed on my bed. It was one of my favourites, an old, well-worn copy of the Greek myths. It had been one of the first books Baba had brought me about the myths. I opened it up and smiled. On the inside of the cover, scrawled in his usual messy handwriting was a message from Baba.

For my darling Clara,

May you grow as wise as Athena, as beautiful as Aphrodite, as strong as Herakles, as inventive as Dedalus and as compassionate as Prometheus.

With love from your Baba.

"AGAIN!" Thanatos said delighted. "SUMMON

72

ANOTHER!"

I stretched out my hand and another book sailed towards me. This one was newer than the first, and was all about the heroes of Greek myth. The front cover had pictures of Herakles, Perseus and Jason, all looking serious with their swords raised.

"PERFECT," drawled Thanatos. "TRY TO SUMMON THEIR WEAPONS."

"No," I said. "Get out of my head!"

I had to fight back. I had to find a way to get him out of my head.

"I SAID," Thanatos growled dangerously, "SUMMON THEIR WEAPONS. DO AS I COMMAND, OR I WILL UNLEASH THE TRUE HORRORS OF MY POWERS ONTO YOU."

I swallowed. Thanatos was the Deity of Death. I didn't want to know what the true horrors of his powers were. I blinked and raised my hand over the book cover.

"GOOD," Thanatos said, apparently pleased that I was agreeing to do what he demanded. "NOW REPEAT AFTER ME. I, CLARA LIU, SERVANT OF THANATOS, CALL UPON THE WEAPONS OF OLD. COME TO ME, AND DO MY BIDDING!"

I did as he said. Nothing happened. The only movement in the room came from the wind coming in from my open window.

"TRY AGAIN," Thanatos commanded. "DO NOT FAIL ME!"

I repeated the instructions, and this time the book cover moved. The pictures swayed about, as if the wind was getting them, and their swords pushed away from them.

"ONCE MORE!" Thanatos cried. "ONCE MORE!"

I did it, and this time it worked. The three swords burst out from the book cover and grew until they were as long as my arm, before collapsing on my bedroom floor.

73

"EXCELLENT!" Thanatos cheered in my head, like a proud teacher. "NOW, COMBINE THEM!"

"I don't know how," I protested, staring at the swords. They were each made of shining bronze, and each of their hilts had jewels encrusted. The sword that had been Herakles' had the most, with rubies and diamonds encircling the entirety of the hilt. Jason's was smaller, with only a few emeralds, whereas Perseus' had only one single sapphire right at the centre of its hilt.

"REPEAT MY COMMANDS," Thanatos instructed. "SWORDS OF POWER, COMBINE INTO ONE, UNITE YOUR STRENGTH AND SPARE NOT ONE!"

I repeated it back, and this time the swords obeyed immediately. There was a blinding flash of light, and when it subsided I saw that the three swords had indeed combined into one. The bronze was shinier, and the hilt had rubies, emeralds, and the one single sapphire from Perseus' sword encrusted into it.

"YOU HAVE DONE WELL," Thanatos said. "IT IS TIME TO MAKE OUR PRESENCE KNOWN TO THE HARVEST GODDESS. I WILL DIRECT YOU. WHEN YOU HAVE GAINED HER TRUST, YOU MUST STRIKE WITH THE SWORD."

I caught sight of myself in the mirror as I stood up and picked up the sword. My eyes had gone the same complete black as Thanatos' had been. When I held the sword, it hummed with power.

"YOU HAVE DONE WELL SO FAR," Thanatos whispered in my head. "NOW WE WILL BEGIN OUR TASK FOR LORD EREBUS. IT IS TIME. WE SHALL DESTROY THE GODS AND RULE THIS WORLD IN THEIR PLACE."

Chapter Eight
Frankie

The night was colder than I'd expected. Seb and I were hurrying down my street, our coats pulled tightly around us, Nicki's jacket clinging to my arm. The cold air helped me get my questions in order for when we eventually found Nicki. Firstly, how had she been able to convince everyone she knew Mum? Secondly, if she wasn't Mum's business partner, who was she? And why had she come round to our house?

"There!" Seb said, as we turned the corner at the end of the street. A few steps ahead of us was Nicki, her head down.

"What do we do?" I asked, as we sped up.

"I don't know," Seb said. "How do we find out who she really is?"

"Follow her," I said quickly. "See where it is she's going. Maybe that'll explain how she was able to make us all think she knew Mum?"

We kept a bit of distance between us and Nicki, careful to hang back in case she turned around. As we walked, I couldn't shake the feeling that there was something odd about what Nicki had done. Not just that had she made Mum think they knew each other, but the fact that whatever she had done hadn't worked on me and Seb.

"Did you notice?" I asked as we turned another corner, this time into a bustling street full of shops, "whatever Nicki did to make the adults think she knew Mum, it didn't work on us?"

"I know," Seb said. "Maybe she thought we'd just believe

what the adults told us?"

That would be so like most adults. They just expect you to accept what they say without question.

"She's stopping!" I said as Nicki made her way towards one of the shops. The windows were full of flowers, and as Nicki approached, I could see she was holding a set of keys that caught the light of the streetlamp that had lit up as Nicky approached. Each key was a different shape, and they all glittered like different coloured jewels in the light.

"Do we follow her in?" Seb whispered as we watched Nicki unlock the door to the shop.

"I guess so," I said. I put on my bravest face and marched forward.

The inside of the shop looked like any other florists. There were displays with carefully arranged bouquets in buckets, a stack of business cards that read NICKI THOMPSON-PALMER – FLORIST TO THE STARS.

"Is this it?' I asked.

"Looks like it," Seb said, pushing a drooping plant out of his hair. "Maybe she is just an ordinary florist after all."

"Then how do you explain what she did to Mum?" I asked, irritated.

"Maybe they really did meet at university. Maybe your mum... I don't know, maybe she did go but dropped out and never told anyone?"

"Are you calling my Mum a liar?" I asked. I don't know why I was getting so annoyed. Maybe it was because I'd wanted Nicki to have magical powers. At least then I could say something interesting had happened to me.

"No!" Seb shot back, going red. "I just mean, everyone has secrets, don't they? Maybe your mum's is that she dropped out of university?"

"Yeah, maybe," I mumbled. "I still want to have to a proper look around."

I threw Nicki's jacket down on the desk that occupied the left side of the room and started inspecting the flowers. There were flowers of all different colours and smells, and at the far end of the shop was a potted plant with low hanging fruits.

"Mhmm!"

"What?" I said turning around to Seb.

"I didn't say anything," he said, inspecting a bright blue flower that changed colour to a pale green as he stared at it.

"Yeah, you did," I said. "You said mhmm."

"No I didn't," he said, still staring at the flower. I rolled my eyes and turned back to the flowers I had been inspecting.

"Mhmm!"

"Oh my god, Seb!" I said turning around. "Will you stop doing that?"

"Doing what?" Seb asked, sounding genuinely confused.

"Mumbling mhmm every time I turn around!"

"I haven't said anything!" he protested hotly.

"Yes you have!" I said. "You said—"

"Mhmm!"

"Exactly!" I said, before blinking. Seb had been looking at me when the last 'mhmm' had been said. And he hadn't opened his mouth.

"There's someone else here," I said quietly.

"Hello?" Seb called out. "Is anyone there? Nicki? You left your jacket at the Sibandas house."

"Mhmm! Mhmm!"

There was the sound of some struggling against something, and the wall behind the potted plant gave a shudder, like someone had banged into it.

"In here!"

Seb and I jumped back in shock. There was someone on the other side of the wall.

"If you can hear me, please help! She's got me trapped here!"

"Is that Levi?" I said, recognising his voice.

"Yes!" he called. "Frankie! You've got to help me! Nicki, she trapped me! I can't get out!"

"Hold on!" I called, looking around the room. There had to be something we could use to get Levi out from behind the wall!

Seb had run forward, and was furiously shoving the potted plant aside. "Help me move this!" he said. I joined him, and together we gave the pot a shove and watched as the plant toppled over and out of it, spilling soil across the floor. Where it had been stood there was now a small opening, just big enough for a key.

"She had the keys," Seb said, looking back towards the entrance of the shop. "One of them had to be for this!"

We rushed over to the desk and started pulling open the drawers, papers and seed samples flying everywhere.

"Where are they?" I said, pulling out an entire drawer and dumping its contents on the desk, I could hear Levi struggling on the other side of the door, and wondered how Nicki had managed to trap him. Most people wouldn't even think about trying to overpower Levi, so how had Nicki managed it? Seb was having no luck either, and I worried that we'd have to try and break down the wall to get to Levi. Mum and Dad would not like a bill for criminal damage to come their way because of me.

"How did she even manage to trap you in there?" I called, still rifling through the desk.

"She's a witch!" Levi called. "She tied me up using her

flowers! I'm being strangled by roots right now!"

"We've got to find that key!" Seb said, tearing open seed packets and spilling them out on the floor.

"How is that helping?" I said, as a packet of sunflower seeds rained down over us.

"She might have hidden them in here!" Seb said. "To stop people from looking!"

"I can assure I have done no such thing."

We looked up. Nicki had appeared out of thin air in front of us, holding the set of keys we had been searching for.

"Now, would you be so kind as to tell me what it is you are doing, rifling through my desk?"

Chapter Nine
Seb

"Let him out!" I said, furiously. "It's against the law to kidnap people!"

"Yeah!" said Frankie, joining me. "Let him out or we'll call the police!"

"There is no need for that," Nicki said. She was smiling, which just made me nervous. Was she planning on kidnapping us too?

"And Mr Carew, do stop screaming back there. You are in no danger."

She waved her hand and the wall pulled back on itself like a curtain. Levi appeared, roots wound around him. They fell away as Nicki waved her hand again, and Levi ran towards her, his hands outstretched. He swore at her, but Nicki didn't budge.

"Do you want me to summon those roots again?" she asked calmly. Levi dropped his hands and stood still.

"No," he mumbled.

"What happened?" Frankie asked.

"She kidnapped me and tied me up!" Levi shouted. "She's a witch, I told you!"

"I am not a witch," Nicki said. "Although, as you have seen, I do possess some control over nature."

"Exactly!" Levi said. "Just like a witch!"

"For the last time, Mr Carew, I am not a witch."

"Then who – or what – are you?" I asked nervously.

"To most people, I am simply Nicki the florist who owns this lovely shop and does a rather good deal on bouquets of roses."

"Who are you to other people?" Frankie asked.

"To my daughter, I am Mother. To my son-in-law, I am a pain in his rear. But you may know me as Demeter."

I burst out laughing. I couldn't help it.

"Yeah right!" I laughed.

"Does it look like I am joking, Mr Morgan?"

That shut me up.

"How do you know my last name? I never told you when you were at Frankie's."

"No, you did not. To learn about you both I had to consult Hestia, the Goddess of the Hearth. It was a dangerous process, and not one I intend to repeat."

"But... you can't be Demeter!" Frankie said, looking just as shocked as I felt. "Demeter isn't real! The Greek gods weren't real!"

Nicki did not look happy about that.

"Is that so?" she asked. "Nobody tells me anything any more. The last I knew, we were all real and living on Earth, but if you have heard differently, I pray you, tell me more."

"But the gods were invented to explain what people couldn't understand, that was all! Everyone knows they weren't actually real people!"

"I find it remarkable," Nicki said, "that you can stand in the presence of a goddess and deny her very existence."

"You're insane!" Levi said. "Frankie's right. The gods aren't real. You probably used mechanics to trap me. Yeah! I bet those roots are just wires that you've painted to look like roots, that's all!"

"If that is what you believe, by all means, please investigate further," Nicki said, a small smile on her lips. She was obviously enjoying this. Levi had made his way over to the roots that had bound him and cautiously picked one up. He ran his hands along it, pulling at the bark that was covering it.

"There has to be a wire!" he said, pulling and pushing at it. "There has to be!"

"Why do you deny what is in front of your eyes?" Nicki asked.

"Because," Levi said through gritted teeth, still trying to find a wire within the roots, "the gods and goddess were not real."

"And yet here I am," smiled Nicki. "As real as any of you. Or perhaps that is it! Perhaps it is you who is not real!"

"Of course we're real!" I said. "We all know we're real!"

"And I know I am real," Nicki said. "I can tell you everything about me, if you like."

"Go on then," Frankie said. Levi was too preoccupied trying to find a wire to pay much attention now.

"My name is Demeter. I am the Goddess of the Harvest, of agriculture, wheat and the grain. For a while, I was goddess of the poppies. I have one daughter named Persephone, who the gods sometimes call Kore. She spends six months in the Underworld, with her husband Hades."

"That's all stuff everyone knows," Frankie said. "It's in all the myths. How do we know you're telling the truth if you're just going to repeat things anyone could tell us about Demeter?"

"You make an interesting point, Miss Sibanda. Perhaps there is an easier way to demonstrate my divine powers to you so that you will believe me. Watch this, and you shall believe me."

Nicki raised her hands. All around the shop, the flowers started to wilt and die, until we were stood in the middle of a pile of petals and broken stems. Without a word, Nicki lowered her hands and began to turn them over and over, and one by one the flowers regained their petals and stood tall, their scents filling the shop again.

"I have just demonstrated to you the powers I hold over nature. I can make plants die and come back to life without a word."

"You have to admit," I said, "that is pretty impressive."

"Thank you, Mr Morgan. Do I take it that you now believe me?"

"Maybe," I said. "I mean, I believe you've got powers, but I don't know about you being Demeter."

"Yeah," said Frankie. "After all, I still think the myths didn't happen."

"It is complicated, I grant you." Nicky said simply. "We – or rather, Zeus and Prometheus – created the first men, but it was their belief, their love of us, that helped keep us real."

"Hold on!" I said sharply. "If we accept that you are Demeter – and I'm not saying I do accept that – then how does Levi fit in to all this? What was he doing here?"

"You could just ask me," Levi said sulkily. His search for a wire had obviously not gone to plan.

"Fine," I said, matching his tone. "How do you fit into this? Are you a god too?"

"I wish," Levi said. "I saw her in Regent's Park this afternoon after I bunked off."

"I knew you weren't in Science!" Frankie said.

"Anyway," Levi said. "She was picking these flowers right, and this police officer stopped her. It's the same one who always tries to bring me back to school, so I made sure to keep out of his way. He stops her, and wants to know what she's doing and she…"

Levi stopped and stared at Nicki. "What did you do to him?"

"Low level hypnosis," Nicki said. "I was not proud of it, but needs must. All the gods have some power over mortals. I simply made him forget I was there and carry on about his day. He will feel a little uneasy for the remainder of the week, but after that he shall be fine."

"So, I followed her here and told her what I'd seen," Levi continued, "and that's when she tied me up and slammed me behind the wall!"

"Actually, I did not slam you. I instructed you to remain where I had left you while I went to deal with your friends. You tried to escape, and I couldn't risk you telling people what you had seen, so I took drastic action. You were never in real danger."

"What do you mean, you left to deal with his friends?" Frankie asked slowly.

"You two," Nicki said. "Levi, in the course of his little tirade against me earlier, happened to mention that you two had witnessed an event involving Erika Pallas. I had to try and remove the memory from your heads, for your own safety."

"You know Mrs Pallas?" I asked, the memory of today's English lesson coming back to me.

"I do. That is why I had to invent a reason to go round to your parents' house, Frankie. After my consultation with Hestia, I knew you were both there. I used a small amount of Mnemosyne's power to make your mother and the other adults believe I knew your mother and had intended for the flowers to do their trick. They should have made you forget."

"So, why didn't they?" I asked.

"Some – very few – mortals have the ability to resist a god's powers. As Mnemosyne has not had cause to use her powers for some time now, I suppose they were weaker than I had expected, and you were able to resist. Now, while you are all here, who would like to help me put the shop back in order?"

None of us put our hands up. Nicki let out a sigh.

"Very well, I shall do it myself. Stand back, against the wall there, go on."

We did as she asked. Nicki – I was still unsure about whether she really was Demeter, so I was still calling her Nicki – raised her hands and waved them above her head. The flowers flew back into their pots, the seeds soared back into their packets and the desk dutifully righted itself and stood as clean as it had when we had first come into the shop. At the back of the shop, the pot we had pushed over stood upright, the soil now neatly back in, and the small plant standing tall with its fruits hanging off it.

I walked towards it, my face transfixed by the purple-red fruit, a low hum coming from them.

"No!" yelled Nicki, making me spring back in shock. I hadn't realised how close to the fruit I was.

"Sorry," I mumbled, backing away. "What's so important about a fruit tree?"

"It is not a fruit tree," said Nicki, coming over to inspect it. "This tree acts as a gateway. It is how, in the winter months, I am able to see my daughter."

"It's a pomegranate tree isn't it?" Frankie asked, coming over and examining the fruit.

"It is," Demeter said. "The fruit that cost my Persephone her freedom."

"Anyone want to explain that?" I asked. Levi tutted.

"Haven't you heard of The Abduction of Persephone?" he asked.

"What's that? A book?" I asked.

"Don't you ever pay attention in lessons?" he asked. I looked at him. Levi Carew, who bunked off school and got kicked out of

85

at least four lessons a day, was asking me if I paid attention in lessons.

"It's the name of the myth about Persephone, Demeter's daughter. Hades, god of the Underworld abducted her and tried to make her be his Queen. When Demeter finally discovered what had happened, she went to collect her. Hades—"

"The lying, two-faced runt," Demeter put in vehemently.

"Yes, that Hades," said Levi with a grin, "agreed to let Persephone go on one condition. She must not have eaten anything from the Underworld."

"A stupid condition," Demeter growled, and for a moment I sensed the goddess within. "Of course she would have eaten something!"

"She ate a pomegranate?" I asked. I still couldn't see why that meant she'd have to stay in the Underworld.

"She ate six pomegranate seeds," Demeter said. "Food that was meant only for the inhabitants of the Underworld. In doing so, she tied herself to that place, and it's ruler for six months of the year."

"And I'm guessing those six months make up autumn and winter?" Frankie guessed.

"They do. I grieved so greatly when she was taken, that my grief affected the world. Now, I refuse to allow her to be stuck down there with him on her own, so I accompany her."

"I bet Hades loves that," I laughed. Nicki gave a wry smile.

"Oh, he is delighted to see me every time."

"So, what happens? Now we know you're Demeter? Are you going to, I dunno, incinerate us?"

"By Olympus, no!" Nicki chuckled. "But you must be brought before the gods. After what happened with Erika in your English lesson and now this, they must be notified that mortals are aware of us."

"Is that bad?" Frankie asked, nervously.

"Not necessarily, no," Nicki said, trying to sound comforting. "Mortals have been aware of the gods before, of course. It's simply a matter of working out what to do with you."

"That sounds... worrying," I said.

"Don't worry yourselves," Nicki smiled. "I'll look after you. Besides, the gods aren't that scary!"

I looked at Frankie. Tonight had gone from slightly strange to full on mental. We'd met a Greek goddess and now she'd told us we would have to meet the other gods and goddess. Could my life get any weirder?

As I was about to find out, yes.

Yes it could.

Chapter Ten
Clara

I did not want to be out this late. It was just asking for trouble. Baba always said that only people who went looking for fights were out late. Yet, here I was. Me, Clara Liu, who was in bed by nine every night and studied so hard she knew the periodic table backwards, was sneaking along an empty street late at night. The sword Thanatos had made me create was strapped to my back. I looked at myself and shuddered. I was in my normal jeans and t-shirt with my bright red converse, but it felt wrong. It felt like someone else. I suppose I was someone else now.

"SHE IS CLOSE," Thanatos whispered inside my head. "SO VERY CLOSE!"

I didn't know where we were. It felt like I was missing huge chunks of the day, as if Thanatos had erased from my head. I looked at my feet. It felt like I was floating above the ground.

"YOU ARE," Thanatos whispered. "SOON I WILL CONTROL YOU COMPLETELY AND YOU WILL SERVE LORD EREBUS."

I could feel my brain becoming foggy. I was losing myself in Thanatos' grip. I tried to fight back, to remember the most basic things about me.

My name was Clara Liu. I attended St Phillip's Secondary School. I was thirteen years old. I had to destroy the gods.

I had to destroy the gods.

"Shut up!" I hissed to myself. I was not going to allow Thanatos to take my mind over, even if he had taken my body.

"FOOL," his voice drawled in my head. "YOU ARE ALREADY FADING. SOON, ALL YOU WILL KNOW IS WHAT I COMMAND YOU."

I had to fight it, but I couldn't. All I could do was walk forward, until I was stood across the road from a florist.

"HERE!" Thanatos screamed in my head. "THE GODDESS IS HERE!"

I couldn't see anyone, but Thanatos was determined. He kept screaming those same words, over and over, until all I could think was that whoever we were looking for was hidden in that shop.

As it turned out, I didn't have to look very hard for her. Within seconds of us arriving in the street, the door opened, and a woman strode out of the shop. Followed by three people I did not expect to see.

Levi, Seb and Frankie were following her, firing questions off rapidly.

"If we're meeting the gods, does that mean we're going to Olympus?" Frankie asked, her voice carrying on the breeze.

"Not exactly," the woman smiled. "You'll see! Now, does anyone have some food on them?"

"How are they not seeing us?" I whispered, but Thanatos was too busy screaming.

"SHE IS THERE! SHE IS THERE! IT IS HER! THE GODDESS OF THE HARVEST!"

"Answer me!" I snapped. "How come they can't see me?"

"YOU ARE HIDDEN IN THE SHADOWS. IT IS A GIFT FROM LORD EREBUS TO ASSIST US IN OUR PLAN."

I didn't want to be hidden in the shadows. I wanted Seb, or Levi or Frankie to see me. To ask me what I was doing here. To introduce me to the woman Thanatos wanted me to hurt, so I could, so I could—

89

"KILL HER!" Thanatos screamed. "YOU MUST KILL DEMETER!"

Across the road, Levi had produced a small bar of chocolate, which the woman Thanatos had called Demeter accepted.

"Stole it off a year 7 this afternoon," he said, earning himself a reproachful look from Demeter. Thanatos kept screaming in my head, and I could feel a sudden rush of anger inside me, like I hated the woman more than anything else in the world.

"Stand back," she said commandingly. "This might go a bit wrong. It's been a while since I tried this."

"STOP HER!" growled Thanatos from inside my head. "STOP HER NOW!"

I felt the sword Thanatos had made me craft appear in my hand, but I didn't move. I was too interested in seeing what was going to happen. Demeter unwrapped the bar of chocolate Levi had offered and let it fall to the ground. It hit the pavement outside the florists with a dull thud. From overhead, a pigeon went to swoop down towards it, but Demeter glared at it and it flew away.

"She likes chocolate," Demeter said. "Says its nicer than all the animals people used to sacrifice to her as an offering."

Frankie, Seb and Levi didn't look as weirded out as I thought they should. Maybe this was how they spent their evenings, with crazy women who threw chocolate on the ground and talked about sacrifices.

"Hecate, hear me!" shouted Demeter. "Accept this offering and answer my call! Come forth to guide us safely to the meeting point of the gods! Come forth! I, Demeter, call to you from across the boundaries of the realms! Come forth to me!"

"STOP HER, YOU STUPID MORTAL!" screamed Thanatos. "IF HECATE INTERVENES, OUR PLANS WILL BE

RUINED!"

I crossed the road towards Demeter, the shadows moving with me. The clouds above the florists had gone dark, and a fierce storm was raining down. Levi, Seb and Frankie had pulled their jackets up in an attempt to shield themselves from the rain, but it didn't seem to be affecting Demeter. She was stood still, her head turned up to the sky, and was still shouting out into the night.

"Hecate, hear me! I am Demeter, Goddess of the Harvest and of the Grain. Answer my call, Hecate!"

I'd crossed over so that I was right behind her. I held the sword up, ready to strike.

"KILL HER!" Thanatos screamed. "SHE IS THERE! DO IT NOW! DO IT BEFORE HECATE ARRIVES AND STOPS US! DO IT!"

"HECATE, COME FORTH!" Demeter yelled, the rain pouring against her. "COME!"

I swung the sword, Thanatos cackling with delight inside my head –

BANG!

There was an almighty crash, and as quickly as it had started, the storm faded away. I dropped the sword in shock, the clang ringing out, it shimmered on the pavement and faded away.

"NO!" roared Thanatos. "WHY DID YOU NOT STRIKE?"

I thought about it. I'd had every opportunity to kill Demeter there and then, so why had I not done it?

"I don't know," I muttered, looking around. The pavement, that only a few seconds ago had looked like the scene of a tidal wave, was bone dry. The only hint that something had happened was the fact that where the bar of chocolate had fallen, there now stood a beautiful woman. She had dark skin and bright eyes that seemed like they couldn't decide on a colour. One minute they were purple, then they were green, then gold. She was wearing a flowing emerald dress, and a bright green emerald hung from a chain around her neck. She smiled at Demeter, and strode over to the bin outside the shop and dropped the chocolate bar wrapper into it.

"Children, this is Hecate, the Goddess of magic," Demeter explained. "Hecate, this is Seb, Frankie and Levi."

Hecate smiled at each of them in turn. Hecate didn't look like how I had imagined her. I'd always thought she'd look a bit like the Wicked Witch of the West, but she didn't. She looked like someone had taken a film star and dropped her right in front of me. She had flowing black hair, and when she spoke, it was like someone had bottled up a ray of sunshine and was letting it out.

"Hello, children," she smiled. "Thank you for the chocolate. You would not believe the awful food they serve down in the underworld."

"You live in the Underworld?" Seb asked, staring at her.

"I sought refuge in the Underworld after we had to flee Olympus. Lord Hades was kind enough to grant my request. It's rather peaceful down there. He's done a lot of renovation work."

Demeter rolled her eyes good-naturedly. "When you've finished singing the praises of my son-in-law," she said. "I need your help, Hecate."

"My help?" Hecate repeated. "It is not often you ask for my help, Demeter. In fact, the last time you asked for my help with something, it led to you abandoning your responsibilities for six months."

"I know," Demeter said. "But you are the only person who can circumvent Hera's boundaries."

Hecate grinned. "Yes I am."

"How?" Frankie asked. "Through magic?"

"Not magic, no," Hecate said. "I am also the Goddess of Boundaries."

"Because they're linked," Levi said sarcastically. Hecate's smile faded.

"Ignore him," Frankie said. "Most people do."

Levi scowled at her, but said nothing. Hecate looked around.

"We need to get to Asfaleia House, and quickly," Demeter explained. "Hera forbids any mortals from entering."

"And you expect me to break Hera's expressed rule, and deposit these mortals right into the House?"

"Something like that, yes," Demeter said. Hecate grimaced.

"Breaking the Ancient Laws, Demeter, it could lead to—"

"I know what might happen," Demeter said. "But I'm sure Queen Hera will understand."

She didn't sound convinced.

"FOOLS," growled Thanatos in my mind. I don't know whether Hecate being goddess of magic meant she could read minds, but as soon as Thanatos spoke, her eyes snapped up and honed in on me.

"You did not introduce this mortal to me, Demeter," she said taking a look at me.

Demeter blinked, shaking her head. "She cannot see us Hecate," she said. "The Empodio makes sure of it."

"I hate to disagree with you, Demeter," said Hecate, sounding thoroughly delighted at being able to disagree with Demeter, "but she can see us."

Demeter's eyes fell on me. "Speak, child!" she called. "Come closer."

I walked over. Demeter gasped.

"The Empodio never fails!"

"Evidently, it has," Hecate muttered.

"Demeter, Hecate, this is Clara," Frankie introduced me. I tried to smile at her, but all that came out was a pained grimace. "She's in our class at school."

"That does not explain how she was able to break through the Empodio," Demeter said accusingly.

"The what?" I asked. Thanatos had finally gone quiet, allowing me to hear my own thoughts at last.

"The Empodio," Hecate said, her eyes never leaving mine. "When Olympus fell, I placed magical barriers around the gods and their dwellings. It means that mortals should never be able to get too close."

"But we made it through," Frankie said. "We were following Demeter, remember?"

Seb nodded. Hecate looked nervous.

"They made it through as well?"

"I may have left the defences lowered," Demeter said quietly.

"For Olympus sake!" Hecate moaned. "Demeter, how many times do I have to tell you, keep your defences up! They could be working for Erebus!"

"They're not!" Demeter protested. "I used the Eisvoli as soon as they came into the shop."

"The eiswhat?" Seb asked.

"Eisvoli," Hecate said impatiently. "It's a power I gifted to the other gods when they came to Earth. It means they can enter a mortal's mind."

"You read our minds!" Frankie exclaimed. "That is so wrong!"

"Why?" asked Hecate, seriously. "You would make use of the power if you had it."

"No I wouldn't!" Frankie said. "It's an invasion of privacy!"

I got the feeling Hecate did not like being challenged. Her greenish glow was getting more intense with each second.

"Stop arguing!" Levi shouted.

That was weird. Levi usually started arguments. He didn't finish them. At least, not without hitting something first. Frankie looked like she had a lot more to say, but held her tongue. Demeter smiled at her gratefully.

"I allowed you to pass through the Eisvoli," Demeter said unconvincingly, "but I put the defences back up once you were inside the shop. So it begs the question, how did Clara get through?"

They all looked at me expectantly. Looking back at my two friends, the school bully, and two Greek goddesses, I knew I could – and should – tell them. I knew how I'd gotten through. It was obvious, to me at least.

Thanatos.

The Deity of Death had lowered whatever defences Demeter had in her possession and had made sure I was seen. It wouldn't surprise me if he'd found a way to make sure Hecate had seen me as well.

"I don't know," I said quietly.

"GOOD," Thanatos whispered in my head. "THE PLAN IS NEARLY COMPLETE."

Hecate's eyes still wouldn't leave me. I was sure she was performing the Eisvoli spell Demeter had used on the others. Any second now she was going to announce that I had the Deity of Death in my head, and then who knows what would happen? She'd probably blast me apart.

"SHE SUSPECTS!" Thanatos barked in my head. "SHE MUST NOT DISCOVER MY PRESENCE!"

"Perhaps there is a reason for Clara breaking through,"

Hecate mused. I tried to stop looking at her eyes, but I couldn't help but be drawn in. I wanted to beg her for help, to tell her about Thanatos, but I couldn't get the words out.

"Only the Moirai will know for sure," Demeter said gently. "And I have no desire to deal with them again."

"The Moirai?" Frankie repeated.

"The Fates," Florian said. "The three old women you see in the myths."

"Like in Hercules!" Seb said. "With the one eye!"

"Not quite," Hecate said disdainfully. "That film is a gross misrepresentation of the gods."

"Hecate's just bitter she wasn't included in it," Demeter quipped. "The Fates are the three old ladies who spin the Thread of Life. The one-eyed women are the Graeae."

"They're the ones Perseus met," I said. "He ransomed their eye for the whereabouts of Medusa."

"Actually," said Levi, "he threatened to destroy their eye unless they told him where he could find the objects that would destroy Medusa."

"No, it was her location," I said confidently.

"WHO CARES?" Thanatos hissed in my head. "JUST GET THEM TO TAKE YOU TO ASFALEIA HOUSE!"

"It was the objects that would destroy her!" Levi insisted. He did not like being wrong.

"It was her location," I said. "I'm right, aren't I Demeter?"

"Well…" Demeter began.

"No, you're wrong. It was the objects!" Levi growled. He was getting irritated now. I felt the urge to push him, to see just how far he would go. That was the most un-Clara like thing I could do. Thanatos was obviously having an effect on me.

"Technically," said Hecate, her eyes still on me, "you're both right. Some myths say it was for the location, some say it was for the objects. Greek myths have been retold so often that things always get changed. Now can we focus? Demeter, are you taking Clara with you to Asfaleia House?"

I held my breath. Maybe, just maybe, if Demeter agreed, Thanatos would leave me alone once we got there.

"I suppose I should," said Demeter thoughtfully. "She's already heard too much about us."

Seb and Frankie grinned at me.

"This is gonna be so cool!" Frankie breathed. "We're gonna meet the gods!"

"I wouldn't get too excited," Hecate advised her. "Meeting the gods only leads to trouble. Just look at what happened to Odysseus."

Seb and Frankie looked so confused at that, I couldn't help but smile.

"From The Odyssey," Levi and I said at the same time. I was beginning to suspect that Levi knew more about Greek myths than he'd ever let on before.

Maybe we had some things in common after all.

"Very well," said Hecate. "I won't be able to get you past the defences outside the House. I'll have to leave you in the field outside."

"Just get us as close as you can," Demeter said encouragingly. "I'll do the rest."

Hecate smiled appreciatively at Demeter and began chanting in Ancient Greek.

"The ground is going to open up," Demeter explained to us. When it does, just walk down. We'll come out in the grounds of Afsleia House."

"Is it safe?" I asked. I had the Deity of Death inside my head,

97

and I was worried about safety? Go figure.

"As long as you're with me, it will be," Demeter said reassuringly. We all watched Hecate with interest. Her chanting was getting louder and more frantic, until eventually the ground beneath us began to crack and crumble, until there was a gaping hole. The rock below had been carved into a staircase, complete with lit torches.

"Is that the Underworld down there?" Florian asked uneasily.

"Not quite," Hecate said. The colour had drained out of her face. I guess ripping a hole into the ground took the energy out of her. "You'll be under the ground but above the Underworld."

I nodded, pretending that what she said made any sense. Thanatos was growling inside my head. I guess he didn't like being near the Underworld.

"Thank you, Hecate," Demeter said, turning to us. "Come along. It's time you met the Gods."

Chapter Eleven
Seb

I've done something stupid things in my life, I'll admit. Skiving off school? Stupid. Trying to prank Raf and ending up drenched in flour? Stupid. Trying to drive Mum's car? Really, really stupid.

But following an Olympian goddess through a hole in the ground to apparently meet the rest of the Olympians? That was single-handedly the stupidest thing I had ever done. A little voice in my head kept telling it was all a lie, and that Demeter was really a crazy woman who was going to kill us all.

That didn't explain how she'd managed to summon Hecate though.

The passageway Hecate had created for us was nothing like what I'd expected. When the ground had opened up beneath us, I'd expected to walk down into a damp, wet cavern, but it was warm and full of bright torches that gave off different colours as you passed. It was like walking through a firework display.

"She's gotten better at doing this," Demeter smiled. "Used to be just damp darkness when you came down here."

"You've been here before?" I asked, trying to keep up with her. She walked far too quickly.

"Oh, me and Hecate go back a long way," Demeter said, slowing her pace. "We visit each other's realms all the time. She even helped me look for Persephone when she went missing."

"Did Hades really kidnap her?" Frankie asked.

"Yes," Demeter said tightly. "He did."

I got the impression Demeter did not like talking about her

daughter and Hades.

"That's awful," Frankie said, easily keeping pace with Demeter.

"Yes, it is," Demeter said. There was a tone in her voice that made me think she didn't want to say anything else about it, and Frankie must have heard it too because she dropped the subject. Levi and Clara were behind us, and I heard him repeating the story of how Demeter had kept him tied up with roots and vines in her shop.

"Well you shouldn't have been such a prat, should you?" Clara said.

I'd never heard her say anything like that to Levi before. I'd never heard her say anything like that to anyone before.

Levi looked like he was trying to find some smart remark to throw back at her, but before he could, Demeter had come to a stop in front of a staircase leading up into the ground.

"We're here!" she called. As she started to walk up the staircase, the ground above us gave a crack and began to split itself open, the dirt folding backwards into itself. The sudden burst of sunlight made me blink, and when I opened my eyes, we'd emerged into the biggest garden I'd ever seen. It looked like the grounds of a castle, with row upon row of flowers, a covered corner with a banqueting table and chairs, a massive fountain with statues dotted around it, and a massive stables full of white horses that were chomping on some hay. In the distance, I could make out a little cottage with a thatched roof and smoking chimney, and I was sure I saw an eagle swooping away above it.

I wanted to say something about how beautiful the place was. Something like 'this place is "Wow, indeed."'

Demeter smiled. "This garden is my pride and joy."

"You grew this?" Frankie said, astonished.

"I certainly did," Demeter said proudly. "All of the gardens on the estate are looked after by me. Well, me and Bill."

Right on cue, an old man appeared from behind the stables. His hair was as white as the horses, and he had a bushy white beard to match. He was dressed in overalls, like the kind a dustman wears, and was carrying a pair of garden shears.

"Ms Thompson-Palmer!" he called, his thick Scottish accent cutting through the air. "You're back!"

"I am! And I've brought guests!" Demeter called, indicating us. "Come and say hello!"

Bill limped over. As he got closer, I could see his face was heavily wrinkled, and he had a scar running between his eyes and disappearing into his hair.

But the thing I noticed most were his eyes. They were a weird mix of brown and black, with a hint of gold.

"Bill, this is Seb, Frankie, Levi and Clara," Demeter introduced us. Bill smiled warmly at us all.

"Friends of the family?" he asked. Demeter made a weird noise in her throat, as if she was choking.

"Some... something like that," Demeter spluttered. "Is Joanna at home?"

"Haven't seen her all day, but I've been busy with the horses," he said. "Harry's home though, if that helps."

Demeter snorted. "Bill, when does Harry being here ever help?"

Bill gave a laugh. "You've got a point," he chuckled. "I'd be careful going into the House. He's been re-arranging the music rooms again. Left all his equipment lying around. I nearly went flying over his guitar earlier."

"Oh marvellous," Demeter said sarcastically. "That's all we'd need, our only groundskeeper to break his legs because

Harry's decided to reconfigure his rooms again. Sometimes I think this family gives you too much trouble, Bill."

"Not at all," Bill smiled. "You know how much I appreciate you all! I really must get back to those horses. It was lovely to meet you!" he smiled at us, before heading towards the stables. As he walked, I could hear him mumbling to himself.

"Family... yeah right," he muttered.

I thought the garden would have been the most beautiful sight I'd see. I was wrong.

Very, very, wrong.

At the end of the garden there was a house. Imagine the biggest mansion you can. Now imagine the biggest castle you can. Now combine them. That would be Asfaleia House. From the outside, it looked like it had at least twenty floors, and the walls were made of a multitude of different materials. The topmost walls were made out of what looked like solid steel, while others were made of seashells, some were made of a blazing red metal, and some of nothing but branches.

"Welcome to Asfaleia House," Demeter smiled. The four of us just stood there with our mouth open. "That's the normal reaction," Demeter laughed. "I probably should have prepared you."

"Normal?" Levi said. He was the only one of us who had remembered how to speak. "You mean other... people like us... have been here?"

"What do you mean, people like us?" Clara asked quietly. Demeter smiled at her.

"Mortals," Demeter said. "Levi means mortals. It takes a while to get used to being called that. One other mortal has been allowed passage to Asfaleia House, and that was a long time ago."

"What happened to him?" Levi asked. "In most of the myths, mortals were never allowed near Olympus."

"That is true," said Demeter. "Most mortals, but there were a few exceptions here and there. As for the only other mortal to be granted access to Asfaleia House, you just met him."

"Bill's mortal?" Frankie asked slowly.

"That's why he called you Miss Thompson-Palmer, isn't it?" Levi said slowly. "He thinks you're just an ordinary florist."

"He thinks we're all just ordinary," Demeter said with a smile. "Bill has no idea who we all are. To him, we are just one mixed up family who own a large house. No more and no less."

"What would happen if a mortal found this place?" Frankie asked.

"They would see an abandoned, boarded-up, burnt out old stately home with an overgrown lawn," Demeter explained. "Now, let's go in."

I had a million questions about why a mortal had been allowed to be the groundsman of Asfaleia House, but I didn't have time to ask. Demeter was already striding through the large double doors and into the House.

Every room inside was designed differently. We passed rooms that looked like the sea, complete with water, rooms so hot that they made us sweat just passing them, rooms full of beauty products and designer clothes, rooms full of grain and wheat, and most impressively, rooms full of actual lightning bolts.

"The War Room is near the top of the House," Demeter said, striding ahead of us. "It's quite the climb!"

On and on we walked, Demeter in front, pointing out the rooms as we passed.

"Aphrodite's apartments," she pointed, as we passed the rooms crammed full of beauty products.

"Poseidon's place." As we passed the rooms made only of sea water. "Every god has a floor dedicated to them, where they can rest and rejuvenate their powers."

We snuck glances at other rooms as we walked. Rooms piled high with books (Athena), rooms full of tools and half-made automatons (Hephaestus), rooms made entirely of flower beds (Demeter).

"Here we are," Demeter smiled. There was just one door now, at the end of a long narrow corridor, and we bundled through it, one after the other, following Demeter.

Our first mistake was going through the door.

Our second? That would be banging into the guy behind the door.

Our third? That would be staring at him. He looked as though he'd been thrown off of a building. His body had been broken, and it hadn't healed well. His face was covered by a thick beard, and what little hair he had was a weird mix of orange, red and yellow, like a fire. He was dressed in the same overalls as Bill, but his were stained with oil, and entire patches of the overalls looked like they'd been scorched by fire.

"Sorry," I mumbled, trying not to stare at him. He towered over us, and his eyes were a funny shade of purple. The more I looked at him, the more I was sure parts of his beard were actually on fire.

"What is the meaning of this?" he bellowed. "Who allowed these minor gods to disrupt us?"

"Minor what?" I asked. The man just stared at me.

"What are you? Water sprites? Nymphs? Dryads?"

"Speak English!" Levi snapped, but instantly shrank in on himself when the man turned his gaze onto him.

"I asked what are you?" the man said, each word coming out

slower than the last, the way some people talk to others who can't speak their language.

"Um, human?" Frankie offered.

"HUMAN?" the man bellowed. "No human could make it through our defences!"

"Correct," said Demeter. "Hephaestus, how about you stop screaming at them, and ask me why I brought them here?"

"You did what?" Hephaestus blinked.

"I brought them here," Demeter repeated. "Allow me to introduce you all to Seb Morgan, Frankie Sibanda, Levi Carew and Clara Liu."

"Hi," I managed weakly. Frankie just waved, while Levi rolled his eyes. Clara looked like she wanted to faint.

"I told you allowing Demeter to mingle with mortals was a bad idea!" a woman said from the other end of the room. She had long flowing hair, bright sparkling eyes and a smile that could have made me do anything.

"Aphrodite, you're just bitter because I wouldn't let you use my flowers in your beauty products!" Demeter snarked. She had taken a seat at the table, and I suddenly felt very alone.

"At least then they'd be useful!" Aphrodite shot back.

"Be quiet!" boomed another voice. This voice was a lot harsher than the others. "If I have to deal with any more family arguments, I shall scream. Hephaestus, sit down for Olympus' sake, I'm bored of your attempts at leadership."

"Yes, mother," growled Hephaestus, taking a seat.

"You three," said the woman who the voice belonged to, "come here. At once."

We moved as one towards her, each of us taking in the sight before us. The woman at the head of the table had short, dark brown hair and eyes that seemed to be constantly moving about.

"Tell me, do you know who we are?" she asked, her eyes never leaving ours.

"Um... a really, really dysfunctional family?" Levi said, grinning. Only one person around the table, a young girl a few years older than us, grinned back.

"Do not encourage them, Artemis," the woman at the head of the table scolded her. But Artemis did not stop grinning.

"We are though, Hera, you must admit it," Artemis chuckled. The other women just frowned.

"We are the Olympians," said the woman Artemis had called Hera. I couldn't help it, I burst out laughing. The whole thought was mental. I'd almost believed it as well! This had to be some sort of practical joke.

"Is something amusing?" asked Hera. It took Frankie elbowing me in the ribs to stop me laughing.

"This is a joke right?" I laughed. "You're all in on it, aren't you? You... You're serious?" I asked, the laughter dying in my throat.

"Extremely so," said the woman. "I am Hera, Queen of the Gods."

"I knew it!" Clara breathed out. "Wait, wait. Let me see if I can work out who the rest of you are."

"Now is not the time to be nerdy!" Levi hissed, but there was no stopping Clara.

"You're Hera, Hephaestus is over there with Artemis," Frankie said, pointing at each of the gods in turn. "The muscle man over there," she continued, pointing out a well-built man with short hair, "must be Ares." The god nodded, barely taking his eyes off the beautiful woman next to him. "The one he's going all puppy eyed over is Aphrodite."

Hephaestus did not look happy about that.

106

"Then next to Artemis must be Apollo, next to him must be Dionysus, and next to him must be Poseidon."

The three men smiled. Apollo winked at Frankie, and I swear she blushed brighter than the sun.

"Hold on!" I shouted, making the gods jump. "You're Harry Jones! From The Boy and His Muses!"

"Guilty as charged!" Apollo grinned. "Singer, songwriter and devilishly handsome guitar player at your service!"

"The who from the Boy and His what?" Hera shrieked.

"The lead singer, from The Boy and His Muses." Apollo grinned.

"You started a band? We have asked you countless time if you have done anything to attract the mortals and you said no!"

"You never said I had to tell you the truth when you asked," Apollo smirked. "Besides, humans have always loved me!"

Artemis groaned and shook her head. "Could you be any more big-headed?" She sighed.

"Don't be jealous, sister. Just because I have excellent taste in music while you have... well, frankly, no taste whatsoever."

Artemis looked ready to punch her brother. Hera tutted, but Apollo was still grinning. Frankie's face was still bright red.

"Then there's Hermes, who—"

"Oh my god!" I breathed out. "Mr Crawford, you're Hermes?"

"Ah. Yes. I should explain," Mr Crawford said.

"You will do no such thing!" Hera snapped. "These mortals are owned no kind of explanation for your presence in their school, Hermes. We do not explain ourselves to those beneath us."

"Wonderful people skills as always mother," Hephaestus sniggered.

"Beneath you?" Levi repeated dangerously. "You think we're beneath you?"

"Naturally," said Hera. "Why would I not think so? You would not exist if it were not for my husband and Prometheus."

"Be that as it may, Queen Hera," Hermes said diplomatically. "I have gotten to know these mortals during my posting at their school. I think I should explain what I was doing there."

Hera sighed. "On your own head be it, Hermes."

"Many years ago," Hermes said, "there was a war. A war for Olympus itself, and we lost. We were forced to flee, but before the final fight against Erebus, the Primordial Deity who led the rebellion against us, there was a prophecy. A prophecy that foretold us of four mortal teenagers who would one day lead the fight back against Erebus. And we believe those four are you four. On Athena's advice, she and I were posted at your school to watch over you and observe whether or not you were the four who might one day see us restored to our rightful home."

I was just about to tell Hermes how insane he was, when a low rumble filled the room.

"Always has to make an entrance, doesn't he?" sighed Poseidon, running a hand through his salt and pepper hair. "You four might want to stand back."

We barely moved out of the way before the door burst open and the same man from my dream appeared in front of us. He was dressed in a faded band T-Shirt and black jeans, with the same dark hair he had in my dream, but now it was cut short. As he strode into the room, I saw that the band on his T-Shirt was Apollo's, The Boy and His Muses.

"Let's get this over with quickly!" he called, taking the seat beside Demeter, who flinched. "Persephone's making pomegranate soup for when I get back. Hello, mother-in-law," he smiled at Demeter, who rolled her eyes.

"It may interest you to know, brother," Poseidon said, "that we have guests."

"Oh. Hello."

I knew instantly that this must be Hades, Lord of the Underworld.

"Hades," Frankie breathed.

"That's me!" smiled Hades. "Lord of the Underworld and King of the Dead, at your service."

"I've already done the 'at your service' speech, Uncle H," Apollo said apologetically.

"Oh," said Hades. "Never mind. Mine's better anyway. As I was saying, Lord of the Underworld and King of the Dead at your service. No, I cannot bring people back to life, no I did not kidnap Persephone, and no, Orpheus did not trick me!"

"Finished?" asked Hera through gritted teeth.

"Almost," Hades grinned. "Finally, yes, I do have a three headed dog, yes, he is housetrained, yes you can pet him. Finished now!"

"Well, that was enlightening," said Demeter. "Thank you so much for joining us, Hades. Our lives are made instantly brighter by your presence."

"Hey, I'm the one who pulls the sun chariot!" Apollo said sulkily. "Why is your life not made brighter by my presence?"

"Sarcasm, dear," said Demeter. Apollo grinned at her.

"Can we get on with this?" boomed Dionysus. "Some of us have actual work to go back to!"

"Sorry," I said. "But what is going on?"

"I would quite like to know the answer to that myself," said Hera. "Demeter, why have you brought four mortal children here? You surely can't be of the same opinion of Hermes and

Athena, that four mortals will be our salvation?"

"Where is here, exactly?" asked Levi.

"A safe point between the mortal world and Olympus," said Poseidon. "Where we meet once a month to discuss our lives and the ongoing search for our King, Lord Zeus."

"Oh my god, it's a family reunion," said Frankie.

"Not quite," said Hades. "Given that the head of the family is not here."

"Where is Zeus?" I asked.

"Not your concern!" shouted Hera. "Back to the matter at hand! Why are four mortal children here?"

At that moment, the door behind Hera opened and Mrs Pallas walked in.

"Oh. My. God!" Clara breathed out.

"You're Athena!" Levi, Frankie and I said in unison. It made perfect sense! Athena was the only goddess not at the table, and now here was Mrs Pallas!

"Oh dear," said Mrs Pallas. "I mean, I don't know what you're talking about! These are just some friends of mine! We meet—"

"They know," said Apollo quickly. "Game's up, Athena."

"Oh," said Mrs Pallas, or Athena. "How did they find out?"

"Through me," Demeter said. "We had a little run in earlier this evening, and I may have revealed all."

"But how did they meet you?" Athena asked. "We're not meant to mix with the same mortals!"

"I know that," Demeter said. "But when we got word that Hades had made contact with Seb, I had to see for myself if these four really were the ones Pythia had told us about! That's why I had to use the charms of Mnemosyne!"

"You used Mnemosyne's charms without my permission?"

Apollo barked. The grin had gone, and now he looked positively furious.

"I did not require your permission, Apollo," said Demeter, testily. "I simply required the assistance of Mnemosyne, who gladly provided it. That is why Rionach Sibanda thinks she has known since university. That is why she thinks we own the florist's together."

"Back to the matter at hand!" snapped Hera. "It still stands that these mortals," she said the word mortals like it offended her "should never have been able to discover our existence!"

"Of course they were going to figure it out!" snapped Hermes. "Especially after Athena insisted on putting photos up in the class! For the Goddess of Wisdom, you can incredibly stupid, Athena!"

"That's what you were arguing about!" Levi said quickly. "You were worried Mrs Pal – Athena – had revealed herself when that old man showed up!"

"Yes, I was," said Hermes. "It's a dangerous business, hiding in the mortal world. We could be discovered at any minute." Hermes looked shiftily around the table, obviously hoping no one else would notice that Levi had mentioned the old man.

No such luck.

"What old man?" Hephaestus asked slowly.

"Father Time," Athena said quietly.

Hera went pale. Hephaestus swore loudly. Even Hades looked nervous.

"The Ancient Decrees ban him from taking any part in the War," Apollo said confidently.

"It does not, however," Ares said, "stop him from influencing them with his powers. If he's sided with Erebus, we're all doomed. Especially if we run the risk of being

111

discovered by mortals."

"We have been discovered," said Artemis. "Or have we forgotten that four mortals are standing in front of us?"

"We should execute them," Hera said, as simply as if she was deciding what to have for dinner. "Hephaestus, do you still have an axe?"

"We are not executing them!" Apollo said, grinning at us. "They could be useful!"

"Useful how?" asked Hermes.

"In the war!" shouted Ares. "Foot soldiers!"

"We are not using mortals as foot soldiers!" Athena answered.

"Or maybe we could explain what's going on?" Demeter barked out.

"She speaks!" said Hades, with a grin. "She actually speaks!"

Demeter glared at him. "Look at them, for Olympus' sake. They look terrified!"

I didn't think we looked terrified, but I wasn't going to interrupt a goddess. From thin air, Demeter summoned four comfortable chairs, and we sat. Instantly, plates of food appeared in in front of us, along with steaming mugs of hot chocolate.

"We are not giving them food!" Hera sighed.

"Too late," Demeter said with a wink at us. "Now, who wants to tell them why we're on Earth?"

Chapter Twelve
Frankie

"Fine, I will," said Hades, standing up and sweeping towards us. I got the impression he rather enjoyed being dramatic.

"There was a war," he began, as I sipped on the best hot chocolate I'd ever tasted. "A brutal, bitter war which—"

"The Titanomachy," Levi said, through mouthfuls of food. When everyone stared at him, he went red. "What? I pay attention in class sometimes!"

"Not the Titanomachy, no," said Hades, evidently irritated that his flow had been interrupted. "Another war. A war between the Olympians and the Primordial Deities."

"Primordial what?" Seb asked.

"Deities," Hades said. "The first beings. They existed before us gods, even before the Titans. They are the personifications of everything around you.

Once we deposed our father Cronus and took power, we had to bargain with them for control. We thought," Hades continued, looking around the table, "that we would have no problems with them. But we were wrong. We thought they had retreated into the shadows, forgotten and alone, but instead they were just biding their time, waiting for the perfect moment to strike. They waited until we had been relegated to myth and legend. Then they attacked Olympus."

"They do not need to know any of this," Hera complained. "All they need to know is that, since you insist on believing that ridiculous prophecy, they are fated to serve Olympus. If you

113

persist in telling them our history I shall—"

"You'll what, Hera?" Hades questioned, turning to face her. "Trick known me into accepting rulership of the Underworld?"

Poseidon suddenly looked very interested in the floor. Hera went quiet, mumbling something that sounded like 'ungrateful swine'.

"I didn't think so," Hades said. "As I was saying, when the Primordial Deities attacked, they unleashed all the hells of Tartarus on us, all at the same time. We put up the best fight we could—"

"Thanks to me!" Ares boasted. Hades scowled at him.

"Thanks to Athena's battle plan," Hades corrected him. "If it had been up to you, Ares, we would have just run in blindly with axes and arrows screaming."

"It would have frightened them off!" Ares growled. "But you decided to go with the brainbox's plan instead, and look where that left us!"

"My plan should have worked!" Athena protested sharply. "It only failed because Zeus abandoned Olympus!"

"Enough already!" Hades interrupted. "Regardless of whose fault it was, our defences failed. But there were some Primordials who stayed loyal to the Olympians. Nyx, Aether, Eros. Even Aion tried to help. But in the end, we had to flee. Not all of us made it off on Olympus."

A thought occurred to me. There were Twelve Olympians, but thirteen chairs at the table, and two were empty.

"Zeus," I said, quietly.

"Didn't you listen to what Hades just said?" Levi asked. "He said Zeus abandoned Olympus."

"Correct," Hades said. "My brother was the first of the Olympians to evacuate. He made sure he was safely on his way

114

down to Earth before any of the Primordial Deities could get near him."

"Then who could've been left?" I asked, but Clara answered before I could give it much thought.

"Hestia. Goddess of the Hearth."

"Yes, Hestia was left behind," Hades said, bitterly. "The Primordial Deities kept her as a hostage, in case we ever attempted to get back to Olympus."

"But you're gods!" Seb said incredulously. "You can do anything!"

"You'd think so," Apollo said. "But even our powers have some limits. The Primordial Deities have given Olympus over to the worst monsters and demons of the Underworld. Even our combined power could not defeat them all."

"So, we're here, on Earth. Living a perfectly normal existence," said Demeter. "We've all got mortal identities and jobs, apart from one layabout," she said, with a pointed look at Hades.

"In case you have forgotten," Hades bit back, "The Primordial Deities swore on the Styx to leave the Underworld alone. By keeping Persephone down there, I am keeping her safe. I offered you the opportunity to come down too, but you refused."

"I like living up here!" Demeter protested. "I have a perfectly marvellous life! No one is going to suspect that Nicki Thompson-Palmer is anything but a florist!"

"You picked a stupid name," Hades said coldly. Before Demeter could answer back, Hera cut in.

"As thrilling as that performance was, Hades, it still does not answer the question of what we are to do about these mortals! We cannot permit them to return to their normal lives, now they know the truth!"

"You can't keep us here!" I argued.

"Yeah, we have rights!" Levi put in.

"Yeah!" Seb said, still focusing on his hot chocolate. "Besides, Demeter told us Bill the gardener is a mortal, and you didn't punish him for finding out!"

I gave him an elbow to the ribs for that. Demeter looked like she'd just received an electric shock.

"I..." she began. The other gods looked furious.

"That is... Bill..." Artemis attempted.

"Bill is allowed..." Aphrodite tried, before also trailing off. Everyone looked uncomfortable.

"There are reasons Bill has been permitted sanctuary amongst us," Hephaestus said gently. "We maintain an illusion of being a normal mortal family around him."

I was just about to tell the gods that there was no way they could pretend to be a normal family, when my head felt like it was going to split open. I closed my eyes to try and get rid of the pain, and instead found myself staring at the walls of a damp, badly-lit cave. A woman with dark hair and a kind, heart-shaped face was sat slumped in a corner. She looked unhealthily thin, and as she tried to stand, I saw that her face was pale.

"Hello?" I said, my voice bouncing off the walls.

"Help me," she whimpered. "You must help me. He has taken the Lord of the Sky. You must find him and bring him home. Only then can you help me."

"Who are you?" I asked, trying to get a better look at her.

"Help me," she repeated. "You must find the Lord of the Sky!"

"Wait!" I called out as the cave began to dissolve around me. "How do I find him? Wait!"

I opened my eyes. I was back in the big room with the gods.

116

Hera was still sat at the head of the table, her eyes on me.

"What is wrong with you?" she asked.

"Headache," I lied. No one looked convinced. I chanced a look at Clara, who had barely said a word since we had got here. Her hot chocolate was untouched, and her eyes were closed.

"Clara!" I hissed, "What's wrong?"

"He's here," she mumbled. "He's here, he's here, he's here."

"Who?" I asked, confused. Her voice was getting louder now, and the Olympians were starting to notice.

"I see no other option but to keep you here!" Hera said, exasperatedly. "We cannot – what in all Olympus is she talking about?"

Clara's voice had gotten louder now, and the ten Olympians were staring at her.

"What is she saying?" Artemis asked, getting up and coming over. "Apollo, I think we're going to need your medicinal skills!"

Apollo leapt up and hurried towards Clara, but he never made it all the way. Without warning, the door was blasted off the hinges, and a hulking Boar stood in front of us all. The Boar's eyes were made of pure fire, and its fur was made of thousands of tiny spears. As it moved closer, I could see the foam dripping from its mouth and trickling down its massive tusks. As it roared, bolts of lightning shot out of its mouth and smashed the windows around the room, sending shards of glass scattering everywhere.

"The Calydonian Boar!" Apollo shouted, grabbing a bow and quiver from thin air. "Arm yourselves!"

All around us, the Olympians were in a panic. Hera screamed "Kill it! Kill the beast!" while Hephaestus roared and launched his axe at it. It barely touched the Boar's fur, bouncing off and rolling away. Apollo and Artemis shot volley after volley of arrows, but just like Hephaestus' axe, they glanced off the

Boar.

"Move!" Apollo barked at us, and we ran for the other door. The Boar must have anticipated our move, because it roared and seized Hephaestus' axe and threw it towards us.

"Get down!" Hephaestus bellowed. We ducked just in time to see the axe lodge itself in the door instead of in us.

"It shouldn't be this hard to kill!" Artemis shouted, loosing another bunch of silver arrows at the boar, who swatted them away like flies. The Boar reared itself onto its hind legs and let out another roar, foam and bolts of lightning flying everywhere. "Boar, heel!" she shouted. "I command you as your creator and mistress, heel!"

That, as you might have guessed, did not work. The Boar launched itself forward, missing Artemis by an inch. As she rolled out of the way, preparing even more arrows, a new voice floated through the room.

"DID YOU THINK I WOULD NOT SET YOU A CHALLENGE, PATHETIC OLYMPIANS?"

I looked at Seb, who had gone white. Levi was shaking. The only one of us who looked calm was Clara.

"THE CALYDONIAN BOAR WILL DESTROY YOU, AS YOU DESTROYED THE TITANS, AND THEN LORD EREBUS WILL RULE OVER THIS RELAM!" the voice said. With a sudden gasp, I realised that it was Clara who had spoken, but not with her own voice. This new voice was cold and sharp, and even the gods looked nervous.

"Who are you?" demanded Hephaestus.

"YOU DO NOT RECOGNISE MY VOICE, HEPHAESTUS?" Clara taunted in the voice that wasn't her own. "I WAS THE ONE WHO VISITED YOU AFTER YOUR DEAR, DARLING MOTHER HAD FLUNG YOU FROM

118

OLYMPUS. YOU SHOULD HAVE BEEN IN MY CLUTCHES. I SWORE I WOULD RETURN FOR YOU ONE DAY, GOD OF THE FORGE!"

"It can't be!" roared Hephaestus. "I imprisoned you myself! I made sure you could never escape!"

"I WAS RELEASED BY LORD EREBUS TO COLLECT YOU ALL! FOR I AM THANATOS, AND I AM HERE TO CLAIM YOU FOR TARTARUS."

Chapter Thirteen
Seb

"Clara!" Frankie screamed as we dodged yet more arrows. "What are you doing?"

"THE GODS WILL PAY FOR WHAT THEY DID TO US!" Clara answered in Thanatos' voice. Her eyes had gone completely black, and they were fixed on the Olympians.

"Thanatos!" Hera demanded, taking a swing at the Calydonian Boar with a long, shining sword. "Release this mortal girl from your control! The Boar cannot be stopped by a mortal, it will tear her apart just as it will us!"

"NO," Clara said simply. "I SHALL NOT RELEASE HER. HER KNOWLEDGE WILL BE KEY TO MY LORD EREBUS RULING THIS WORLD. AS FOR THE BOAR, IT WILL NOT HARM THE ONE WHO IS IN CONTROL OF IT, WILL IT, ARTEMIS?"

Artemis, still shooting arrow after arrow grimaced.

"Artemis, what's he's talking about?" I yelled, as we dodged the Boar again.

"I was the one who sent the Boar to Calydonia," Artemis explained breathlessly, weaving her way underneath the Boar's massive paws. "The King had not honoured me, so I wanted to punish him. It took an entire league of heroes to bring it down, but it was instructed to never harm the person who sent it!"

"So what do we do?" Frankie screamed, dodging more lightning and flames from the Boar as it swiped at the gods.

"Run!" Levi answered, wrenching Hephaestus' axe free and

throwing it aside. He was just about to pull the door open, but the Boar was quicker. A bolt of lightning smashed into the door, sending Levi sprawling across the floor.

"Levi!" Frankie screamed, darting towards him. He was flat on his back, and his eyes were shut. I went to run towards them, but the Boar shot another bolt of lightning at me, and I flew through the air as the floor became an inferno. I could just make out the Olympians fighting against the Boar as I landed with a thud on the floor behind it. Sitting proudly on its back was Clara, and she was still speaking with that cold voice.

"YOU WILL FALL AT MY HAND!" she shrieked, laughing manically. "AND I SHALL BE REWARDED!"

I tried to think, to remember what I knew about the myth of the Calydonian Boar. Artemis had said it had taken an entire league of heroes to defeat it, but how had they done it?

"Artemis!" I yelled, hoping she'd hear me. "How did the heroes defeat this thing?"

Artemis looked over at me. She was badly bruised now, and had an open cut on her forehead that was bleeding. I was so concerned with killing the Boar, I didn't even notice that her blood was gold. She shouted something back, but at that moment the Boar let out another roar and leapt towards her.

That's when I saw it. On the Boar's great hide, there was one spot that wasn't covered by spearheads or spikes. If I could get a good shot at it, we might stand a chance of getting rid of it!

"Aim for the hide!" I screamed, but the roar of the Boar was louder. There was no chance of me getting any of the god's attentions while the Boar thrashed and swiped at them.

"Frankie!" I shouted, barely able to hear myself. "Throw me an arrow!"

Frankie looked up from where she was still crouched over

Levi, who was trying to sit up. I hoped he'd be all right. After all, not many people can say they've been blasted off their feet by the Calydonian Boar, can they?

Frankie did as I asked, grabbing a discarded silver arrow and tossing it to me. It was sharper than I'd expected, and in tiny lettering it read 'Property of Artemis. Theft will result in pain'.

"What are you doing?" Levi yelled, still trying to sit up without collapsing. "You can't fight that thing!"

"Watch me!" I shouted back. Without thinking, I ran towards the behind of the Boar and slammed myself into it. As I did, I shoved the arrow into its hide and was thrown back as it roared in agony.

"WHAT HAVE YOU DONE?" screeched Clara, looking down at me with those completely black eyes. Her face was twisted in rage, and her voice was even colder now.

I looked up at the Boar, desperately hoping my plan had worked. The Boar was thrashing and writhing about, trying and trying to pull the arrow out of its hide. The same golden blood that was flowing down Artemis' face from her cut was now pouring out of the spot where the arrow was lodged in the Boar. It took the gods a few seconds to realise, but when they did, nothing could stop them.

"The hide!" Artemis yelled. "Aim for the hide!"

Arrow after arrow, axe after axe, sword after sword, every weapon they could find made its way to connect with the Boar's hide. Finally, after one final thrust of Poseidon's trident, the Boar collapsed and vanished, as if it had never been there. The only evidence that we had just fought off a mythological Boar was the cut on Artemis' face and Clara, who had been thrown from the Boar as it thrashed around, and was now running for the door.

"Stop her!" Hera yelled, sheathing her sword. "Do not let her escape!"

I made a dash to catch Clara, but she turned on me with those dark eyes and raised her hands. Instantly I was sent backwards, colliding against Hephaestus who pulled me to my feet.

"DO YOU THINK, HERA," spat Clara in Thanatos' voice. "THAT I WILL ALLOW MYSELF TO BE CAPTURED BY YOU? YOU, A FORMER QUEEN WHO THREW HER OWN SON FROM OLYMPUS? YOU, WHO FLED YOUR PALACE IN THE HOPE OF SAFETY ON THIS DUMP OF A PLANET?

"Seize her!" Hera demanded. Hades was the one who made to move towards Clara, but as soon as he did, Clara let out a mirthless, cruel laugh.

"WHAT WILL YOU DO, KING OF THE UNDERWORLD?" She laughed. "WILL YOU CAST ME DOWN TO TARTARUS IN THIS FORM? WILL YOU SET YOUR FURIES ON ME? WILL YOU TRY TO DROWN ME IN THE STYX? YOU AND I BOTH KNOW THAT A MORTAL BODY, ESPECIALLY A YOUNG MORTAL, COULD NEVER WITHSTAND THE HORRORS OF YOUR UNDERWORLD. NOR COULD IT WITHSTAND THE HEAT OF HEPHAESTUS' FORGES, OR THE TIDES OF POSEIDON'S SEAS WHEN HE IS THERE. THERE IS NOWEHRE YOU CAN SEND ME WHERE THIS MORTAL BODY WOULD NOT BE INSTANTLY DESTROYED."

I looked at the gods, who looked... defeated?

"Thanatos is right," Aphrodite said. "There's nothing we can do."

"Nonsense!" bellowed Dionysus. He had spent the best part of the fight trying to protect his glass of wine, and when he spoke, he swayed on the spot. "Send the girl to Tartarus, Hades! If she was stupid enough to let Thanatos take control of her, so be it!"

Levi and Frankie looked ready to punch Dionysus, but Athena stepped in.

"Let her go," she said. "But I swear, Thanatos, if you harm her in any way, you will feel the force of all Olympus come crashing down on you."

Clara let out that cold laugh again. "THE FORCE OF OLYMPUS? THE FORCES OF OLYMPUS ARE CONTROLLED BY MY LORD EREBUS, YOU HAVE NO POWER OVER THEM ANY MORE. I SHALL LEAVE THIS PLACE AND NONE OF YOU SHALL TRY TO FIND ME. IF YOU DO – IF ANY OF YOU TRY TO SO MUCH AS GUESS AT WHERE I HAVE GONE, OR WHAT MISSION I HAVE UNDERTAKEN FOR LORD EREBUS, I SWEAR ON STYX HERSELF, I SHALL UNLEASH MY FULL POWER ON THIS MORTAL FORM."

And with that, Clara vanished.

Chapter Fourteen
Frankie

"Where did she go?" I asked, shakily. "She just vanished!"

"It's a power possessed by most immortals," Hephaestus said softly. "We can come and go with ease."

"But you can find where she is, right?" Levi said. Hephaestus shook his head.

"I'm afraid not. We have no way of tracing where Thanatos may have forced her to go. The only person who could do was Zeus, and as you can see, Zeus is not here."

"Who was controlling Clara?" Seb asked. He had slumped down into one of the seats Demeter had provided for us. I guess taking down the Calydonian Boar must have taken it out of him.

"He said he was The Lord of Death?" I said. "But I thought Hades—"

"No," said Hades. "I am Lord of the Underworld and King of the Dead. Thanatos is something else entirely. He represents all the fear and anguish at death. I merely rule over those who have passed on. I sit on a throne and observe them. Thanatos takes pleasure in death."

"That's horrible!" I said.

"It is the natural order of things," said Hera, pragmatically. "There are gods and deities for everything. Even death, my dear. But Thanatos being out of Tartarus is not a good thing."

"What is Tartarus?" I asked, going to sit beside Seb. Levi stayed on his feet, casting nervous glances around, as if the Boar could reappear at any moment.

"The deepest, darkest pit of the Underworld," Hades said. "Somewhere even I do not venture if I can avoid it. It is the place Zeus imprisoned the Titans after the Titanomachy. We also used it to keep some of the Primordials in check, including Thanatos. If Tartarus has freed him—"

"Wait, so Tartarus is a person too?" I asked.

"He is," said Aphrodite who was combing her hair out of her face, ignoring the carnage around her. "He guards Tartarus as well as being Tartarus. Make sense?"

"Not in the least," said Levi.

"Good. It's better if some things don't always make sense," said Artemis. She had finally noticed that she was bleeding, and was had taken a seat to allow Apollo to tend to her.

"Anyway," Apollo cut in, "we imprisoned some of our most troublesome Primordials in Tartarus. When Erebus, the Primordial of Darkness took Olympus, he freed an awful lot of them."

"And I'm guessing Thanatos being on Earth isn't a good thing?"

"Your guess would be correct," said Ares. "I still think you should've let me pulverise him when we had the chance!"

"Fighting is not always the answer," said Dionysus. "I suggest we all have a drink together and work through our problems."

"Can I ask," I said, sounding a bit braver than I felt, "if there are meant to be Twelve Olympians, and Hestia is the only one who the Primordials took hostage, why is there still only ten of you? Shouldn't there be eleven?"

"Ah. Yes." said Athena. "I wondered when we would get to this question."

"Zeus is missing," said Demeter. "Has been for about twenty

126

years."

"How can a god go missing?" asked Seb.

"That's what we've been trying to find out," said Hades.

"For twenty years?" said Levi. "And none of you have solved it?"

"Obviously not," said Hera, angrily. "Otherwise he would be here, wouldn't he?"

I could feel Levi getting annoyed, and part of me wanted to see him take on the Queen of the Gods. After all, she had suggested executing us. But I'd have to wait, because no sooner had Levi prepared a reply, then the door opened, and a young woman stepped in. She had flowing brown hair, a kind face and was dressed in a long blue dress. She had the kind of eyes that you couldn't stop looking at. One minute they were blue, then green, then brown, then purple.

"What is it now?" groaned Hades. "First we're interrupted by mortals, then a Boar from Hell, than Thanatos and now what?"

"Ignore him, Pythia," said Apollo smiling. "What is it?"

"My Lord, a new prophecy has been declared."

"Who's that?" I whispered, but not quite enough for Apollo not to hear.

"This lovely lady," Apollo said, winking at the woman, who blushed, "is Pythia, or, as she's better known, The Oracle of Delphi. Teller of prophecies, follower of me, and a really good maker of coffee."

Pythia laughed. After hearing Clara's cold laughter, it was nice to hear a genuine laugh again.

"Speak, Pythia, Oracle of Delphi. Declare your prophecy before the gods," Apollo instructed. "And mortals," he added quickly. The Oracle cleared her throat, and said in a loud voice:

Lost to the winds in years gone by

127

The hunt must begin once more for the Lord of the Sky
Found not by Olympians, hidden away
Three mortals will find him or be tempted astray
Trapped in the concealed rock of grief
Death himself they must defeat.

The Oracle collapsed into a chair, her words ringing out.
"What was that?" Levi asked.
"That," said Apollo gravely. "Was Pythia's latest prophecy."

Chapter Fifteen
Levi

"Okay…" I said quietly, looking at Pythia, who was breathing hard. "But what does it mean?"

"Well," said Apollo. "It sounds like the hunt for Zeus needs to begin again."

Like everyone else in the room, Apollo's eyes were trained on Frankie, Seb and me.

"You… you don't think the three in the prophecy are us, do you?" Seb asked.

"Makes sense," said Hephaestus. "You three had to have found your way in here for a reason. Must be you."

"But you said the reason was because of the other prophecy, the one about reclaiming Olympus!" I said.

"That was about four mortals," Hera said. "As one of your group has had her mind claimed by Thanatos, I consider it highly unlikely that it can refer to you."

"Thanatos hasn't claimed Clara's mind," Frankie said coldly. "We'll find a way to free her."

"I doubt it," Hera said simply. "Very few people survive meetings with Thanatos."

"We'll just have to make sure Clara is one of the few who does survive then, won't we?" Frankie said, glaring at Hera.

"On your own head be it," said Hera. "Back to the matter of your quest to find my husband—"

"This is insane!" I interrupted. "We're three thirteen-year-olds! We can't go on a hunt for Zeus! We can barely make it through a day at school!"

"You will have help," Hera said, although she looked like she wanted to agree with us.

"Hold on!" Frankie said. "Don't we have to, like, accept the quest or something?"

"Nonsense," said Hera. "You have been chosen by the Oracle. Her decision is final."

"But... what about our parents? They'll be worried!"

"I shall deal with that," said Hermes. "I shall fix their memories so that they believe you are on a school trip. Apollo, let Mnemosyne know that I shall be calling on her."

Apollo rolled his eyes. "Sure, just use my Muses' powers, it's not like we've got a sell-out show to do tomorrow, what does it matter if they're all half-asleep because you've kept them up all night siphoning their powers?"

"You haven't been able to find Zeus in twenty years!" Seb protested, ignoring Apollo's whining. "What makes you think we'll be able to do it?"

"The Oracle has ordained it so," said Hera. "You will find the Lord of the Sky and you will return him here."

They all made it sound so normal. I suppose for them, it was. But we were three Year 8 kids who had barely spent any time together before today. How were we going to work together to find the King of the Gods when the Olympians hadn't managed to even get a hint on where he might be in twenty years?

"Come on," said Artemis with a smile. "I'll get you kitted out."

"Kitted out?" I repeated.

"You're going to need armour, and weapons. Who better to get them for you than the Goddess of the Hunt?"

The armoury was incredible. It was on the very top level of

Asfaleia House, behind a set of heavy metal doors that Artemis had told us were made of Stygian steel.

"Those doors were forged by Styx herself," Artemis explained as we waited for them to swing open. "The combined forces of Erebus, Cronus and Lord Zeus themselves couldn't get through it unless we wanted to do. And believe me, Erebus' lot have tried. Repeatedly."

The inside looked like someone had raided an army base. Camouflage kits were hung up ready to be worn, extensive battle plans were laid out across three adjoining tables, and one wall had a detailed map of London, with red and blue dots splattered across it.

"What do these dots mean?" Frankie asked.

"Ah, the old Zeus board," Artemis said, coming to stare at it with us. "You'll need a copy of this. It's every known location Zeus liked to frequent before he disappeared. The red dots are placed we've checked. The blue are the ones we never got around to."

"I don't understand," Seb said. "If you guys have been looking for Zeus for twenty years, why hasn't one of you found him?"

"A good question," Artemis smiled. "We are limited in what we can do on Earth. We cannot cross into each other's personal domains without permission, and with the amount of time we spend arguing, it's no wonder we don't get anywhere. Poseidon will not allow Athena into his seas to search, she will not allow him into her universities to search. I have my tribes of women to keep checking in on, and Apollo has busied himself being a Rockstar. Soon, the Hunt for my father fell to the wayside. I cannot say it to Lady Hera, but I suspect some of my fellow Olympians have rather given up."

"But couldn't you phone the police and report him missing?" I asked. Artemis shook her head.

"Lady Hera will never allow it. It would bring too much attention to us. That is why we are relying on you."

We all looked at each other. Artemis sounded so worried about Zeus as she explained why they hadn't been able to find him. We all nodded. We might be thirteen, and we might be mortal, but we were going to do our best to find him.

We spent at least an hour just walking around the armoury. Every kind of weapon, from swords to maces to cannons was lined up ready to be used. Artemis had found armour for each of us, which fit to us perfectly.

"The armour adapts to your shape," she explained, helping Seb tighten the straps of his breastplate. "So, even if you grow a few inches while you're searching for Zeus, it'll still be a perfect fit."

It still felt strange, having a girl who looked barely older than us telling us about armour, but given how today had turned out, I wasn't going to start questioning it.

"I'd suggest picking an edged and a melee weapon," Artemis said with certainty. "Makes it a lot easier when you're caught unaware. That way, you get to choose how much damage you want to inflict on your opponent."

Each of us ended up with swords. Seb had picked the one Artemis called Efkinitos, or Agile. It was long and sharp, and looked like someone had gone way overboard on shining it. When he picked it up it glittered, the light hitting the silver.

"Be careful with that one," Artemis said. "Always remember to clean and sheath your sword after a fight. A fool parades about with his weapon, but a warrior knows it is only to be used in the gravest of circumstances."

Seb nodded and put his sword into the black scabbard Artemis had given him. It was strapped to his side, and when he walked away with it stuck to him, it looked like it had always been born there. For his melee weapon, Artemis had suggested a dark brown club, which she had made light and easy to carry. Seb had gripped it tightly, and when he swung it, he smashed an ornate pot into hundreds of tiny pieces.

"Sorry!" he blushed, trying to grab the pieces of what had been the pot.

"Don't worry about it," Artemis had said, smirking. "It's only thousands of years old."

Seb nearly passed out at that. Artemis just laughed.

"Mortals. So easy to wind up. Frankie, you're next."

Frankie had selected a bow and arrow made of the thinnest wood I had ever seen. Each arrow had brilliantly blue feathers attached to their end, and the heads looked sharp enough to cut through anything.

"A girl after my own heart!" Artemis chorused, admiring the bow. "I know this bow," she said, tracing her hand along it. "We used to call it Peto. In English it means fly. I have only ever known it miss one target, and that was because he jumped into his blasted sun chariot and rode away."

"Doesn't Apollo drive the sun chariot?" Frankie asked.

"Let's move on," Artemis said, dodging the question.

Artemis handed Frankie what looked like a smaller, sharper version of Hephaestus' axes. "Use these with extreme caution," she said. "They were made by Hephaestus himself and contain the power of his forges. One hit will feel like a thousand suns are burning inside the target."

"Cool!" I said. Artemis did not seem to share my enthusiasm. When I stepped up to choose my weapons, she looked uneasy.

"Think very carefully, Levi. Once you chose a weapon, you are giving it your service."

I looked around, trying out a few different swords before settling for a slim sword with a wickedly sharp point.

"A very good choice," said Artemis. "<u>Atsali</u>, or Steel."

"Because it can cut through steel?" I said hopefully.

"No," Artemis answered with a laugh. "Because it is an exceptionally hard sword to beat. Those who have come up against it have not often found themselves the winner of that fight."

I went with a lance for my melee weapon. Artemis raised her eyebrows.

"Not many people pick the lance. I trust you will find a good use for it."

She handed it to me and turned her back to us. She was facing a rack of shields that went all the way up to the ceiling. She handed one each down to us, making sure they matched our weapons. They all looked the same, but were each inlaid with a different image of the gods. Seb's had Apollo, Frankie's had Hephaestus and mine had – to my disgust – Hera.

"These shields will react to your opponent," Artemis explained. "If they are stronger than you, the shield will become tougher. If they are weaker, it will become weaker."

"Why would we want it to become weaker?" I protested.

"Because, Levi," Artemis said, "that would make it a fair fight. And I insist on fair fighting."

I didn't think Thanatos would insist on fair fighting, but I let it drop. I was too preoccupied with the weapons Artemis had given us. She'd shrunk my lance down until it fit in my pocket, and Frankie and I both had the same black scabbards that Seb was wearing. We looked like kids playing dress up, but I felt like

I had so much power inside me at that moment. Bring on Thanatos, I thought to myself.

"Well," said Artemis brightly, leading us out of the room and towards the grounds we had run through. "Only one thing left. Your transport!"

She was taking this in her stride, and it made me relax a little. It seemed like Artemis had faith in us, so maybe we did stand a chance at finding Zeus after all.

As we made our way outside, we passed Hera, who looked at us as if we were something disgusting she'd scraped off of her shoe. I didn't feel so confident after that.

"Don't worry about Hera," Artemis whispered. "She's just not that fond of mortals."

"Why not?" Frankie asked. She was clinging onto her shield with all her might, as if she expected a monster to appear out of nowhere and attack us.

"Let's just say Zeus hasn't been the most loyal of husbands," Artemis whispered to us. "He has quite the liking for mortals, and Hera does not approve of it."

"But I thought," said Seb, "that all the gods were carrying on with mortals? Isn't it, like, a rite of passage or something?"

Artemis laughed. "Hera is the Goddess of marriage. She's the only one of the gods with a husband or wife who doesn't cheat on them!"

"Do you have a husband?" I asked. When Artemis looked at me, I realised I was blushing and looked away.

"I do not, no," she said. "Myself, Hestia and Athena are eternally sworn off men. I shall never marry, or have boyfriends."

"That sounds so depressing," Frankie whined.

"Perhaps, to a young mortal it does," Artemis said. "But I have found it perfectly enjoyable."

Frankie didn't look like she agreed, but she didn't say anything else as we finally made our way out into the massive grounds. The night had turned dark, with the inky sky having only a few clusters of stars.

"There was a time," Artemis said sadly, "you could walk around these grounds and see all the different constellations. Not any more, not since Zeus disappeared. Some say," she said, drawing closer to us, "that the Constellations Council, the beings that help us govern on Olympus, were taken with him when he vanished. I would consider it a personal service if you would try to find them for me."

We all nodded. We were already trying to find the King of the Gods, so surely finding a few missing Constellations couldn't be any harder than that.

I don't know what you'd expect, when you hear the word transport. Maybe a taxi, or a train?

I'm going to guess you would not have expected a brilliantly white winged horse.

"Meet Pegasus!" Artemis beamed as the horse flew down and stopped in front of us, allowing the goddess to stroke him.

"He's beautiful!" Frankie said in awe.

"He's the real Pegasus!" Seb said, equally amazed.

"He has wings!" I said.

"And he can talk!" said Pegasus, making us all jump back. "They don't put that in the myth, do they?"

"Pegasus!" Artemis said, frowning. "What have we said about frightening people?"

"Sorry," the horse mumbled.

"Pegasus is going to be your ride. He'll take you wherever you need to go, provided you give clear instructions. None of this drop me anywhere business. Have you got everything?"

We all did one final check in our backpacks. Along with our weapons, armour and shields, Artemis had given each of us a smaller, folded up version of the map from the Armoury. It contained the names of the different places the gods had never gotten around to searching, and on the back were small polaroid photos of the different forms Zeus liked to take when he was on Earth.

"I can't give you any ambrosia," she explained. "It's food for us gods, but to you mortals it'd be like swallowing poison. You'd barely last a minute with it in your system."

"That's encouraging," I muttered.

"You're going to have to keep your wits about you," Artemis said seriously. "Don't get into any fights if you can avoid it. Don't try to take on any monsters that you cross. Don't think that just because you've undertaken a quest for us that it makes you powerful. You're still human, you're still vulnerable to injury and worse."

"Thanks for the pep talk," I said, but Artemis was in the mood for jokes.

"I'm serious," she said. "I want you three – you four – back here in one piece. Find Zeus, and then let him deal with Thanatos. I know you want to free your friend from his control, but you have got to tread carefully. I'll give you my blessing. It should allow you to survive any encounters with monsters, but even that can fail sometimes. So, for the last time, be careful."

We nodded our agreements. Artemis gave us one last look, that couldn't decide between serious or grinning before vanishing in front of us. We clambered onto Pegasus, with Seb at the front, me at the back and Clara in between us, and let our hands sink into his white coat.

"Hold on tight," said Pegasus.

137

I tried not to look down as we took off. Pegasus started at a run, and then with a whoosh, his wings unfurled and started whipping up the wind as we climbed higher and higher into the dark night sky.

We were on a flying horse.

In the dead of night.

Going to try and find a missing Olympian god.

What was my life turning into?

Chapter Sixteen
Clara

"NO!"

I didn't know where Thanatos had made me disappear to. I had felt a strange feeling in my bones, like someone was twisting each of them in turn, and then I'd landed face down in a dark and dingy room, at the foot of a massive throne in which was sat a tall, pale man with stringy black hair and eyes of bright red flame. The walls of the throne room shook every time the man shouted, and he was doing a lot of shouting.

"How did you manage to lose the Boar? I instructed it to destroy the Olympians! They should be dead, dead, and rotting in Tartarus, but they are living! Because you failed!"

"I DID NOT MEAN TO FAIL YOU, MY LORD," I said, Thanatos' voice rushing out in a desperate plea. "BUT THE MORTALS DISCOVERED THE BOAR'S WEAK SPOT. THEY WERE ALBE TO DESTROY IT. I COULD NOT STOP THEM."

"You could not?" snarled Erebus, Lord of Darkness, from his throne. He was shrouded in darkness from his neck down, and as he swayed in his seat with anger, the throne was swaying with him. "Or you would not?"

The little light that had been in the room disappeared as Erebus spoke. The only light was coming from the bright red fireballs where his eyes should have been.

"I TRIED MY LORD," Thanatos whimpered in my voice. "BUT I COULD NOT HAVE ANTICIPATED THAT THE

MORTALS WOULD DISCOVER—"

"You did not try hard enough!" Erebus' anger burst out of him as he waved his hand. In an instant I found myself slammed against a wall, the stones cracking around me. An old woman hurried towards me, her white hair flying behind her. She bent down and pulled me towards her, stroking my hair.

"Leave her, Hestia!" demanded Erebus. My vision had gone blurry, and I was sure I was bleeding.

"She is a child!" spat Hestia, Goddess of the Hearth. She sounded regal and commanding, but Erebus hardly reacted to her. "She cannot handle the same level of pain as Thanatos!"

"Then he should have picked a worthier host, shouldn't he?" Erebus said. The anger was gone from his voice. He just sounded bored now. "Picking a female was bad enough, but picking a female child? What was he thinking?"

"THEY WILL COME," I said, but it wasn't my voice. It was the voice of Death himself. Hestia let go of me and recoiled. I realised she looked scared, and that scared me. I could deal with Seb, Frankie and Levi looking scared of me when Thanatos took over, but seeing a Goddess scared was a whole different thing.

"THEY WILL COME FOR YOU, MY LORD, AND YOU WILL BEG FOR MY AID," I croaked out in Thanatos' high voice. "YOU WILL BEG ME TO UNLEASH DEATH UPON THEM ALL."

"Me? Erebus, Lord of Darkness and Master of Olympus, who made even the Olympians quake with fear! What would I need with a being like you, Thanatos?" Erebus drawled, still sounding bored. I raised my eyes to try and take in his appearance, but all I could see were those burning eyes.

"YOU WILL BEG FOR MY AID WHEN THEY FIND HIM. PYTHIA HAS DECLARED IT. THEY WILL FIND THE

KING OF OLYMPUS, AND RESTORE HIM TO POWER. WHEN THEY DO, MY LORD, YOU WILL BEG ME TO VISIT HIM. YOU WILL BEG THANATOS TO VISIT DEATH UPON THE KING OF THE GODS."

"Find Zeus?" laughed Erebus mockingly. "Those gods couldn't even find their own thrones!"

"THEY WILL FIND ZEUS," I continued, still speaking with the voice of Death. "AND WHEN HE DOES, YOU WILL BEG ME TO SUMMON THE MOIRAI AND HAVE HIS THREAD CUT!"

"Enough!" roared Erebus. "I will not listen to any more of your nonsense. You will return to Earth, and you will capture them. If you fail me, Thanatos, I shall disintegrate this pathetic form you have chosen, and seal you back in Tartarus myself."

Wordlessly, he swept from the room and I could feel myself being pulled back to Earth. I wondered, as I fell, whether Erebus had seen the same thing I had.

Three cloaked old women surrounding him, with a heavy pair of scissors at his throat.

I wondered if he knew what it meant.

If he knew how long he had left.

Chapter Seventeen
Seb

Working out where to start looking for the King of the Gods who hadn't been seen in twenty years was not an easy task. The blue dots on the maps Artemis had given us were far apart, and although there wasn't many of them, deciding which ones were the most likely to be used as hiding places was proving difficult. Zeus seemed to be just as happy in a London pub as he did in a Scottish university.

"Where would he go if he wanted to hide?" I asked, trying not to look down as Pegasus reared up and gained more height. With the way Frankie was clinging on to me, I fully expected to wake up tomorrow with bruises across my chest.

"Look at what Artemis has written next to the address in Edinburgh!" Frankie shouted over the noise of Pegasus' wings.

Next to a blue dot high up the map, Artemis had scribbled something down in messing, winding handwriting. It took me a few minutes to work out what it said.

12 Circus Lane, Edinburgh – HE LIVED HERE!

"Pegasus!" I called down to the flying horse, "can you take us to 12 Circus Lane, Edinburgh?"

"Zeus's old place!" Pegasus whinnied. "Hold on tight!"

I didn't think I could hold any tighter, but I let my hands sink into Pegasus' coat and braced myself as he rose even higher up into the sky.

So, it turns out Pegasus had a death wish. At least, that's how it felt. He would rise up as high as he could on our way to Circus

Lane, before diving straight back down towards the ground, pulling up at the last second to avoid splattering across the motorway. Somehow, we had made it out of London without Pegasus hitting the motorway, and were zooming over the M1 with barely an hour behind us.

"How are you flying this quickly?" I shouted down as we sped on.

"Distance is different for me!" Pegasus shouted back. "You wouldn't understand! Let's dive again!"

Any attempt at refusing that suggestion died in my throat as Pegasus flew down again, pulling up at the last minute.

"Will you stop doing that!" roared Levi, who was gripping onto Frankie as if his life depended on it. Which I suppose it did. I didn't dare look down as we sped on, until eventually Pegasus neighed loudly.

"Welcome to Edinburgh!" he called. I let myself look at the city below us. Lights twinkled on from the houses, and directly below us was a tiny little street made up of picturesque houses and a winding cobbled street. Pegasus took another nosedive and Frankie let out a scream as he hurtled towards to the street. At the last moment he spread out his wings and landed gracefully, trotting along a few steps before stopping completely. We hopped off, each of us still clad in our armour that Artemis had provided, all holding our weapons.

"What happens if you're seen?" Frankie asked Pegasus, who was happily munching on some flowers that were hanging out of window box outside one of the houses.

"People'll think I'm a horse," Pegasus said. "I keep the wings hidden, plus the gods make sure mortals don't see too much. Haven't you ever wondered how they've been able to live on Earth for so long?"

I'd been so overwhelmed by everything that had happened that it hadn't even occurred to me to ask how the gods had lived on Earth undetected for so long, but I wasn't going to admit that to Pegasus.

"Go on then," said the horse. "Have a look around! I'll be here when you're finished."

With that, Pegasus went back to happily munching on some flowers, leaving us stood outside the door to number 12, Circus Lane.

The door, like the rest of the outside of the house, looked faded.

"It looks empty," I said, pressing my face against one of the windows. The inside of the house was deserted, with no light. I had to press myself right against the window to even make out the shape of a small sofa and armchair inside.

"Do you think," said Levi, "that that might have something to do with the fact Zeus hasn't been seen in twenty years?"

I rolled my eyes at him. Now wasn't the time to get into an argument with him, as much as I might have wanted to.

"How're we going to get in?" Frankie asked, looking around. "Do you think one of the neighbours might have a spare key?"

Before she'd even finished asking the question, Levi had gotten to work, using the blade of his knife to force the lock open.

"That's breaking and entering!" Frankie hissed. "It's illegal!"

"So call the police," Levi hissed back. "Or, you could come inside and have a look around."

Frankie and I locked eyes. We both knew breaking into someone's house was wrong, but at the same time, we'd been given a job to do, and if that meant we had to bend the rules a little bit, then surely that was okay?

As soon as we got inside the house, it was obvious nobody had been here for a long time. There was a thick layer of dust over every surface, and mountains of mail littered the floor. We split up, Frankie and Levi taking the upstairs and me downstairs. The living room was small, with a cracked black sofa and armchair, and what looked like a never-ending row of bookcases along the wall. The opposite wall was crammed full of photos of a tall man with grey hair and a short grey beard, stood next to different Olympians. I fished around in my pockets for the photo Artemis had given us of Zeus and realised that he was the man in the photos. There was a large one of him and Athena at what looked like her university graduation, and smaller ones of him with Hephaestus outside an old-fashioned blacksmiths shop, with Ares outside a gym, with Apollo in front of a massive poster for The Boy and His Muses, with Artemis in front of a wildlife reserve, with Hermes outside a running track, and with Dionysus outside a theatre. Looking back at the massive photo of Zeus and Athena, I realised there would be no prizes for guessing who the favourite child is in that family.

"Anything down here?" Levi asked, walking into the room with Frankie.

"This was definitely Zeus' place," I said. "Look at the photos."

Levi and Frankie came and stood beside me, each taking in the photos of Zeus and his children. The frames were all made of gold, and inlaid with images of eagles.

"Zeus' sacred animal," Levi said. I still couldn't believe he'd paid any attention to Athena's lessons.

There was a sudden sharp knock on the door. We all jumped back and looked towards the windows. There a figure outside.

145

"Don't answer it," Levi said confidently. "They'll go away when they realise no one's here."

"We're here," I said. Now it was Levi's turn to roll his eyes at me.

"Whoever's out there doesn't know that, do they?" he said. "Just keep quiet."

"What if it's the police?" Frankie whispered. "What if someone's reported us for breaking in?"

"Nobody saw us," Levi said. "There's nobody else around. It's probably someone asking for money for charity."

There was another knock, louder and more insistent. This time the person on the other side of the door called out.

"Open up! This is the police!"

"I'll go," I said, swallowing hard. I made my way into the hallway and breathed in. I had to think of a lie that wouldn't make it sound like we had broken into an abandoned house.

I threw open the door, expecting to see a police officer.

But it wasn't a police officer on the other side. The man was dressed in a sharp black suit, the kind a film star might have worn in the fifties. He had white hair down to his shoulders and when he looked at me, I saw the same dark eyes that Clara had had at Asfaleia House.

This was not going to go well.

"Good evening," he rasped. His breath smelt like the stale cigarettes and beer I'd smelt once when I'd walked past a pub late at night. I tried not to gag. "I am the owner of this house, and I would like to know what you are doing inside it," he said, trying to sound pleasant. I backed away.

"Oh, we were just looking for something," I said. "We didn't realise someone lived here."

The man did not look convinced. His face had gone hard,

and he started walking towards me. "Why are you here?" he asked.

"That's none of your business," I said, deciding to try a different tactic.

Big mistake.

As I went to move, he held out a hand and I felt myself flying backwards. I landed against the stairs with a crack and could feel blood dripping down my neck.

"Not again," I muttered, remembering how hard I'd sailed through the room back at Asfaleia House.

"Oh, I don't think so, mortal," the man snapped. "You will answer my questions, or you will die."

I knew it would be pointless to try to get up and run. By the time I'd tried to stand back up, he'd have knocked me back again.

"What are you doing here?" he asked, his hand poised ready to strike again.

"I told you," I said. "Looking for something."

"Do not lie to me, mortal," he said menacingly. "I know you have consulted the gods."

"We're looking for something," I half-lied. I wasn't about to tell him we were looking for Zeus. I wasn't stupid.

"Looking for what?" the man asked, towering over me.

"I don't know. The gods said we'd know when we found it."

There was a shout, and suddenly Frankie and Levi were in the hallway, their weapons drawn.

"Wonderful!" the man grinned. "More mortals to kill!"

It was the perfect distraction. As he turned to tackle Frankie and Levi, I threw open my rucksack and pulled out Efkinitos and charged. I felt woozy, but somehow I kept my balance.

The man, whoever he was – and he certainly wasn't mortal – anticipated my attack, turning at the last second and bringing his own sword down onto mine. The black blade seemed to be made of volcanic ash, and when it hit my sword, the sparks were blinding.

Levi tried next, bringing his own sword down, but the man was faster. From thin air he pulled another sword out and smashed it against Levi's. Together we slashed and hacked at this stranger, but he blocked our every move.

I looked at Levi, both of us struggling to match this man's moves.

A single thought occurred to us both.

Run.

We both pulled the same move at the same time. We pulled back suddenly, making our attacker lose his footing. Behind us, Frankie loosed an arrow, which hit him square in the chest.

Nothing happened.

No scream, no ichor dripping from the wound, no sudden collapse.

He just laughed.

We had no time to react before he repeated the first trick he had used on me, sending the three of us slamming down to the floor.

"Who are you?" I croaked, the breath knocked out of me.

The man let out a laugh. It was the most horrific sound I'd ever heard.

"I am Tartarus," he said. "Keeper of the Keys of the Underworld and jailer of monsters. And you, mortal, are about to die."

Chapter Eighteen
Frankie

I am going to die in Zeus' abandoned house. I'm going to die at the hands of the worst prison in the Underworld. This is not how I imagined dying!

"Tell me, little mortals," snarled Tartarus, advancing on us. "Did you really think you stood a chance against the Primordials? Did the gods even tell you why we fought them? Did they even explain why they had fled to this pathetic world?"

None of us spoke. Whether that was because we couldn't, or because Tartarus was asking questions we all had, I don't know.

"Did they even tell you who you were looking for?" he cackled, clearly enjoying his moment in the spotlight.

"Zeus," I managed to say. My lips were bleeding from where he had slammed us to the ground.

"Zeus!" bellowed Tartarus. "That pathetic old man! He was the first to run from Olympus, and now they want him found! Oh, you poor foolish mortals. You have no idea what you have gotten yourself into. It is no matter. I shall enjoy killing you. I hope you'll enjoy your prisons in Tartarus!"

We couldn't fight. Tartarus had made sure that when we fell, our weapons skidded out of reach.

We were going to die.

Tartarus loomed over us, his eyes as black as night and his face twisted in a smile. He raised his hand and the ground began to creak and crack from under us. I let out a scream as Levi and Seb scrabbled backwards, trying to get away from the chasm

Tartarus had opened up beneath us.

"One more move and I will rip your throat out," growled another deeper voice.

I didn't know how Hades knew we were in trouble, but I figured that question could wait. He was stood right in front of us, in tattered black jeans and a black hoodie, his long hair tied back in a ponytail.

"Lord Hades," Tartarus spat. "Move aside."

"Nah," said Hades. "I'm happy here thanks."

"That was not a request, Olympian. Move aside, or I will destroy you too, just as I am going to destroy these children."

Hades laughed. The King of the Underworld actually laughed.

"Tartarus, Tartarus, Tartarus," Hades chuckled. "Let's be serious here. You know as well as I do that if you so much as think about destroying me, I will rip you apart with my bare hands and then reassemble you to do it all over again."

Tartarus said nothing. Hades turned to look at us and winked. None of us winked back. We were too stunned.

"These mortals—" Tartarus began, but Hades cut him off.

"Tell me, Tartarus, what did you actually think would happen here, mate? I mean, did you think that if you stopped these guys from completing their quest, there wouldn't be trouble?"

"They are mere mortals!" screamed Tartarus.

"Who have been given a quest by Pythia herself. Do you fancy going back to her and telling her you killed her chosen ones?"

"The oracle does not scare me," said Tartarus defiantly. "I have no fear in me!"

"Then why are you backing away from me?" Hades asked,

darkly. "If, as you say, you have no fear."

"I am the Lord of Tartarus, the deepest pit of the Underworld! I have no fear!" Tartarus screamed. He sounded desperate, like he was trying to prove something. Hades turned to face us. His face had gone hard and when he spoke it was in a low, controlled whisper.

"Close your eyes," Hades instructed us. "Now."

We did as we were told. I have no idea what Hades did, but whatever it was, Tartarus screamed with terror, and when we opened our eyes, he was gone.

"What did you do?" Seb asked, pulling me to my feet.

"Something I have not done in a long time," Hades said simply. "I scared Tartarus to death."

"Gods... I mean Primordial Deities, they can die?" Levi asked. Hades shook his head.

"No, but I reduced Tartarus to a state of such terror that he'll not bother you again. At least, not for a while."

"How did you know we were here?" I asked, but the answer came quickly. Pegasus swooped down, his white wings beating against the night sky.

"I thought you might need a hand!" he called, coming to a rest in front of us. "So I went and got Emo Boy."

"I've told you not to call me that!" Hades said. "Just because I happen to like wearing black, and once attended a My Chemical Romance gig—"

"Could you two argue later?" Levi said, already climbing back onto Pegasus. "We're no closer to finding Zeus and I don't want to hang around here longer than we have to."

"Oh, that was the other thing I needed to say!" said Hades. "But if anyone asks, I didn't say a word, and you worked it out on your own. The prophecy mentions the rock of grief. It was the

151

name we gave to a hideout of Erebus', back when he was launching his attack on Olympus."

"He hid on Earth?" Seb asked, shocked.

"Sort of. He had hideouts and battle stations throughout all the realms, even in the Underworld. We thought they'd been closed up when he took over Olympus, that's why we never searched any of them. But then the prophecy... Pythia does not give prophecies often. The prophecy you heard back at the House was her first in several years, and the first to ever mention a Rock of Grief."

"But why wouldn't Pythia have mentioned it to you before?" Levi asked.

"I cannot speak for her," Hades said. "The Oracle has always been a mystery to me. But she has her reasons for things, and for some reason she's chosen to mention it to you. I cannot be sure of why she has mentioned it, but you could do a lot worse than checking out the Rock."

"Where is it?" I asked.

"That's the problem. The gods never access it from the mortal realm, not in the same way you would, anyway. When it was taken over by Erebus, we could just appear there to try and fight him, we never used mortal travel to get there."

"In other words," Seb said disappointedly, "you don't know where it is, do you?"

"Not exactly," Hades confirmed. "Erebus had made a deal with Pontus, the old Lord of the Sea, to gain his support in the uprising. The Rock of Grief had belonged, at one point, to Pontus. We scoured this land after the uprising trying to find it. The closest we ever got was Aphrodite and Poseidon hearing a faint trace of Zeus along the Jurassic Coast. But we never got any closer than that. Just a faint trace."

"We have to start there then," I said quickly. "Why didn't you ever try to search him out again?"

"I have had...other matters to occupy my time," Hades said hotly. "I cannot spend all my time searching for my brother, There are other gods who could – who *should* have been searching all the time!"

"Let's not turn this into an argument," Seb said. "Look, Hades, we'll start on the Jurassic Coast. It's got to be worth a shot, right?"

"Right," the King of the Underworld agreed. "Good luck, and whatever you do, don't tempt the Fates!"

There was an almighty rumble and in a flash, Hades vanished, leaving behind a patch of scorched ground where he had stood.

"Is it just me," I said, "or is anyone else getting the feeling the gods are a bit rubbish?"

Chapter Nineteen
Antigone

"They are close," I whispered. "Your brother has seen to it that they know you are here." I stepped away from the brazier and sat down. The man opposite me did not say a word. I looked up at the ceiling of the cave we were trapped in. I knew the curse well enough by now. No more than two people could visit me at any one time. As soon as the mortals arrived, the cave would split itself in two, and I would be sealed off again.

"I wish to remain with you," said Zeus. "It is not fair that I be rescued and you left here in this cave."

"It must be so, my Lord," I said. The King of the Gods had spent twenty mortal years trapped with me. I knew how to get him to agree to things. "You are needed. If Pythia's prophecy about these mortals is correct, they will be the ones to win your home back for you. They will need your counsel, your leadership. What use would they have for me?"

"There are many things you could advise them on, Antigone," said Zeus sympathetically.

"Like how to disobey your King and be trapped in a cave?" I smiled. Zeus sighed.

"Did I ever punish Creon for that?" he asked wistfully. "I could have turned him into something. A fly maybe. Or a rat."

"You saw to it that Medea took care of him," I reminded Zeus.

"Ah yes. How is Medea these days?" Zeus asked.

"She's doing well," I said. "Still running her marriage

154

counselling business with Jason."

I was just about to bring Zeus up to speed on all the heroes and heroines he had lost touch with when there was a rumble from outside.

Someone was opening the cave.

"Behind me!" Zeus commanded, getting up. Even after twenty years, he had not lost any of his powers.

The rock that covered my cave rolled aside and a young girl entered.

"Who are you?" boomed Zeus. "State your name!"

"YOU DO NOT RECOGNISE ME IN THIS FORM, DO YOU, ZEUS?" said the girl in a voice that made my blood run cold.

"Thanatos," Zeus spat. "What do you want here?"

"NOTHING MUCH," said Thanatos in his high, slimy voice. "THE MORTALS YOUR WIFE SENT ARE ON THEIR WAY. IT SEEMS THEY HAD A LITTLE HELP ESCAPING TARTARUS' PLANS FOR THEM. I WONDER, HOW COULD HADES HAVE DISCOVERED THEIR LOCATION?"

"How the ruddy hell should I know?" barked Zeus. "In case it escaped your notice, Thanatos, you've had me trapped in this cave for twenty years!"

"YOU HAVE HAD COMPANY, HAVE YOU NOT?" Thanatos snarled.

"You leave her alone!" Zeus demanded, taking a step towards Thanatos.

"WILL YOU ATTACK ME IN THIS FORM, ZEUS?" he drawled.

"Face me as yourself!" Zeus snapped. "Or are you a coward?"

"I CANNOT," Thanatos said. "SINCE OUR LAST

ENCOUNTER, I HAVE BECOME… UNABLE TO EXIST IN MY TRUE FORM."

"HA!" boomed Zeus. "The Deity of Death, forced to exist using host bodies! It's pathetic!"

Thanatos – or rather, the girl he was controlling – looked angry now.

"YOU WOULD CALL ME PATHETIC?" he snarled. "YOU, WHO I KIDNAPPED AND HAVE KEPT AS PRISONER FOR TWENTY MORTAL YEARS?"

"You betrayed my trust!" Zeus yelled. "You made me believe you were on my side!"

"AN EASY DECEPTION," Thanatos said coldly. "AND LOOK WHERE IT GOT YOU. TRAPPED WITH ANTIGONE IN THE CAVE THAT SHALL NEVER SEE DAYLIGHT."

"What are you doing here?" I said, stepping out from behind Zeus.

"THE MORTALS ARE COMING. THEY MUST BELIEVE THEY HAVE FOUND ONLY ZEUS."

"No!" Zeus boomed.

The curse. It made sense, really. When Creon had sealed me up in the cave, long before Pontus had claimed it as his own and given it over to Erebus, he had ensured no mortal could see me. I was to die alone here, but Zeus and the other gods took pity.

"But even we cannot undo all curses," Zeus had explained on his first visit. "We can come to you, Antigone, and keep you company through your imprisonment, but only one at a time. The magic that contains you will not allow more than one immortal to be here with you at one time."

I wished, even now, that that had been all it was. But we had learned there was more to it.

Apollo and Artemis had come to visit me together, and it had

156

gone horribly wrong. The cave had shook and roared when they entered, and I had been forced to hide up against the wall as parts of the cave broke off and flung themselves at the gods.

"No more than one!" a voice had screamed out. Apollo had fled, and as soon as he was out of sight, the cave had settled.

"What was that?" I had asked, shaking.

"What was what?" Artemis had asked cheerily, sitting down by the brazier. "I've got so much to tell you, Antigone!"

I had realised over time that when Apollo and Artemis had tried to enter together the cave hadn't just blocked Apollo's entry, it had made Artemis forget that he was ever there in the first place. If more than one immortal visited me at the same time, they would forget where they had been and what they had been doing.

I had to hand it to Thanatos, it was a pretty good plan. After all, now that Zeus was trapped here with me, any other gods who came to rescue him would never get in, or remember why they had been here in the first place.

No wonder no one had come for him.

The cave gave an almighty shake as Thanatos laughed.

I knew what was coming. Thanatos wanted to make sure the cave's curse was resetting itself. I smiled one last smile at Zeus, before the walls of the cave shook once more and I found myself alone again, with only my brazier for comfort.

Chapter Twenty
Levi

After Hades' little disappearing act, we were back in the air on Pegasus in no time.

"Where to?" he called as we took flight, Edinburgh becoming a dot below us.

"Somewhere along the Jurassic Coast," I called back. "The rock of grief, apparently!"

Pegasus whinnied. "Not there!" he called back.

"Why not?" Frankie called.

"Bad place!" Pegasus neighed. "Not somewhere I want to visit!"

"But Hades said that's where Zeus might be!" Seb said. "It's the only lead we've got!"

"Bad place!" Pegasus repeated. "Very bad!"

"How about a deal?" I shouted, an idea forming in my head. "Drop us off near the Cave and you don't have to stay? You can fly away as soon as you've dropped us off!"

"He's our only ride!" Seb protested, but I could tell Pegasus was considering the deal.

"We'll figure something out!" I reasoned. I had no idea what we would figure out, but right now my one concern was getting us there.

"Deal!" Pegasus neighed, and we shot off into the night sky, the three of us screaming as Pegasus resumed his routine of kamikazeing it towards the motorway and pulling up at the last second.

The night was cold, and Pegasus' wings were constantly whipping up the wind in front of us. I tried not to focus on the fact we'd nearly died twice already, and started forming a plan in my head for when we got to the rock of grief. I was already expecting another fight with a mythological monster, but expecting it didn't mean we'd be able to fight it. The fact Seb had managed to stab the Calydonian Boar was dumb luck, and Hades had been the one that saved us from Tartarus. If he hadn't shown up, we'd be making our way down to his kingdom now. There was no way the three of us would be able to take on a full grown monster and come out of it alive. I pushed the thought out of my head and focused on the views below us as we passed over towns and countryside, edging closer and closer towards the Jurassic Coast.

By the time we made it to the Jurassic Coast – or more specifically, the part of it where Pegasus thought rock of grief might be – dawn had broken.

"I never get tired of seeing him pull that chariot," Pegasus said. I swear, if a horse could sound wistful, he did.

"Who?" I asked. I remembered something about a Titan with a sun chariot, but I had no chance of remembering his name.

"Apollo," Pegasus whinnied. "Took Helios' job after... well, he drives the chariot now."

I got the feeling there was more to that story, but I wasn't going to ask. Not yet anyway. We had more important things to worry about, like finding the King of the Gods.

"So, that's the rock of grief?" asked Frankie. Pegasus had deposited us on the coastline near Dorset. A faded sign had read:

MAN O' WAR BAY.

"It's around here somewhere," Pegasus said, uneasily. He sounded nervous.

"It's just a bit of coast," Frankie said. "Why are you so nervous?"

"Bad energy!" said Pegasus, who was trotting uneasily on his hooves. "Monsters have been here!"

"Well, that's encouraging," I said sarcastically. "At least we'll be in good company."

"Don't joke about it!" Pegasus whinnied. "Danger is here!"

And without another word, our only way out of here took off and flew away.

"What do we do now?" Frankie said, watching as Pegasus flew further and further away.

"We look for a cave. And if we're lucky," said Seb, "we find the King of the Gods."

Chapter Twenty-One
Clara

"THEY ARE CLOSE!" whispered Thanatos. "PREPARE YOURSELF!"

The cave had shuddered and shook as Thanatos cast his curse. Antigone had been swallowed by the rock, leaving me facing Zeus, who still looked like he wanted to blast me apart.

"I SAID PREPARE YOURSELF!" Thanatos screamed in my head. I focused on what I had to do. Summon the sword made of pieces of Herakles, Perseus, and Jason's weapons. I closed my eyes, picturing it in my hand. I felt it appear, and looked down. It looked sharper than it had last time I'd used it.

"YOU WILL DESTROY THOSE MORTALS," Thanatos snarled. "AND THEN I WILL CONSUME YOU. YOUR EVERY THOUGHT WILL BE OF HOW TO SERVE LORD EREBUS. YOU WILL BECOME HIS FAITHFUL SERVANT."

"Why me?" I said, fighting back against his voice.

"IT WAS FORETOLD," Thanatos reminded me. "LOOK UPON YOUR DESTINY, CLARA LIU."

The brazier in the corner of the cave burst into dark black flame. Zeus gave a start and recoiled. As the smoke rose up, an image began to form. I saw Pythia, the beautiful Oracle of Delphi, in a massive temple. Carvings of Apollo were etched into the pillars and walls around a central brazier, at which Pythia was stood. Before her was a man I recognised instantly. He had fiery eyes and long hair, and the shadows of the room clung to him like a cape.

"What do you see?" Erebus demanded.

"It is not clear," Pythia said. "A mortal girl with knowledge of our legends... she will be instrumental in maintaining your power. Lose her to the gods, and she will be key to your downfall, Erebus. Sway her to your side, and you will be victorious. Allow no one but your closest advisors to contact her. Do not trust the one you call friend. If he controls her, you will lose her forever."

"Nonsense," Erebus laughed. "A mortal girl could never help me keep power. What do the mortals know of my overthrowing of Olympus?"

"Find the girl," Pythia repeated. "Find the girl and sway her to your cause. If you do not, your days on Zeus' throne—"

"IT IS MY THRONE!" bellowed Erebus like a spoilt child. Pythia barely reacted. She just blinked and carried on with her prophecy.

"If you do not find this girl and sway her to your cause, your days on Zeus' throne will be numbered."

The image of Pythia and Erebus flickered away, until all that was left was burning coals.

"There's no proof Pythia means me," I said defiantly. "Any mortal girl could have knowledge of the Greek myths. We all get taught about them."

"KEEP WATCHING," Thanatos crowed. "YOU WILL UNDERSTAND."

The brazier burst back into life. The flames licked higher and higher, the smoke dancing around us until the image before me was clear. It was my house, back when I was a little girl. Mama and Baba were stood in our garden, Mama sipping tea and listening to the radio, Baba with his nose in one of his mythology books.

"You know," Baba was saying, "I've been thinking. I might

buy Clara some of those books we saw about mythology."

"Which ones?" Mama asked.

"All of them," Baba smiled. "You never know, she might like them. You could end up with two mythology experts in the family!"

Mama laughed. "That's all I need," she chuckled. "Don't you go starting debates about Zeus and Hera's marriage over dinner again."

"That only happened once!" Baba protested. "And Mr Jackson enjoyed the debate!"

"It was a dinner party," Mama said with a smile. "And you spent all night talking about myths!"

I was so caught up in watching Mama and Baba that I only noticed the other man in the garden as the image was fading. It was Cronus, the same crooked smile and white hair.

"What the—" I began.

"WATCH," Thanatos instructed me.

The image began to shimmer and change. It was a few weeks later at my tenth birthday. I was sat in the living room, wrapping paper all around me as I opened the different presents my family had brought me. I remembered this like it was yesterday. Baba had made good on his plans, and brought me the mythology collection I still had today. Again, Cronus was there, hidden in the shadows, that sick grin on his face.

The image began to shimmer again, and I was seeing my first day at St Phillip's. I was in English, on that same table at the back. Seb and Frankie had just sat down. They looked just as nervous as I did.

"Hi," Seb smiled at me. I tried to return the smile, but all that came out of my mouth was a squeak.

"I'm Seb, and this is Frankie. We're in the same form as

you."

"Hi," I managed to get out. "I'm Clara."

They had been the first friends I had ever made at St Phillip's. If you listened to some of the other kids at school, they were my only friends. They weren't, but the more I thought about it the more I realised they had, without me ever really noticing, become my best friends. I missed them. I wished I could get a message to them, to tell them where I was and that I was with Zeus. Maybe they'd summon the gods. Maybe they could help get Thanatos out of my head.

The image shimmered away, and this time I was making my way through the Science corridor at school. It was busy, with students piling out of the different classrooms. I knew what was coming. Without warning I flew to the ground, smacking my face off the floor. Levi was stood next to me, snickering.

"Whoops," he said, smirking. "Didn't see you there."

That had been the day I vowed I would never talk to Levi Carew. And yet, here in this cave, with the Deity of Death in my head, I really wanted to see him. Mainly so he could punch Thanatos in the face. But also because, ever since we'd met Demeter, I'd started to suspect that maybe there was a little bit more to Levi. Maybe he wasn't all bad. I looked at the image, and as I had expected, hidden in the swarm of students was Cronus.

"DO YOU UNDERSTAND NOW?" Thanatos asked. I nodded.

"Cronus has been spying on me," I said as the image shimmered away to nothing.

"For thirteen years Cronus has been scouring this pathetic planet looking for the mortal girl Pythia prophesised."

The brazier spluttered out final image. It was Cronus, and he was bent low in front of Erebus' throne.

"My Lord," he said breathlessly. "I believe I have found the girl from the prophecy. Her name is Clara Liu."

I heard Cronus reel off every detail he had learnt about me. How Baba lectured on mythology. How I had become just as obsessed with the myths as he was. How I – in Cronus' words – was friendless and lonely, and how I would welcome the honour of serving Erebus.

"You have done well, my servant," drawled Erebus. "Go to Earth. Look for this girl. When you found her, I shall send my noblest follower to take control of her."

"I am noble!" whined Cronus. "I am the one who has followed her for thirteen years!"

"You cannot involve yourself in my plans, remember?" Erebus said without pity. "Ever since your son overthrew you, he has seen to it that you are no more than an eternal time keeper. Go to Earth, Cronus, former Lord of All. Go, would-be-king. Go, and find that girl. When you succeed, former-master-of-all," Erebus taunted, "send for Thanatos. Then you will return to me. I have need of your time powers."

Cronus nodded and was gone. The image in the smoke drifted away. Finally, I understood why Cronus had been at school. It had nothing to do with Athena, or Hermes. He was looking for me. Erebus believed I would be key to making sure the gods could not get back onto Olympus.

I knew what I had to do then. I had to fight against Thanatos with all the strength I had. I had to get him out of my head before Erebus could use me.

But how?

"Lord Thanatos," came the high reedy voice of Tartarus. He appeared in front of me and collapsed in pain, writing on the floor. His suit was smoking, and his face was deathly white.

"Surely it is better to allow me to find these mortals—"

"YOU HAD YOUR CHANCE!" I snapped in that voice that wasn't mine. "YOU FAILED LORD EREBUS! YOU ARE LUCKY TO BE ALIVE, TARTARUS! IF I WERE SAT ON THE THRONE I WOULD HAVE BLASTED YOU APART!"

That shut him up. Tartarus backed away, hiding himself in the shadows of the cave.

"IT IS TIME" Thanatos whispered in my ear. "THEY ARE HERE! SUMMON THE CATOBLEPAS!"

The last thing I remember was a rumbling sound and what felt like an explosion from under the ground as a monster with shaggy fur and blood red eyes erupted from the ground and let out a low grumble. It took off out of the cave at a charge, leaving a gaping hole in the ground where he had burst out of.

The man chained to the wall groaned. "No…" he whispered, his voice croaky and horse. "Spare them…"

Tartarus gave him a kick. "Silence, your Highness," he mocked, aiming another kick at the man. I winced and looked away.

"YOU HAVE DONE WELL, CLARA," whispered Thanatos in my ear. "THE CATOBLEPES WILL MAKE SHORT WORK OF YOUR FRIENDS. WHEN THEY ARE NOTHING BUT DUST, WE WILL TURN HIM ONTO OUR PRISONER."

He looked at the man in chains and laughed. "TARTARUS, TAKE GOOD CARE OF OUR GUEST. THE KING OF OLYMPUS MUST BE KEPT COMFORTABLE, DON'T YOU AGREE?"

Tartarus joined in the laughter. I looked over at the man in chains, and the battered, bloodied face of Zeus stared right back at me.

Chapter Twenty-Two
Seb

We stood staring after Pegasus, who was flying away at breakneck speed. He was little more than a white dot in the sky when we eventually turned to look at each other.

"So, this is where Zeus might be," I said. It didn't look like somewhere a god might hide out in. It just looked like an ordinary beach.

"That's what Hades said," Levi answered. "Look, before we try and find him, don't you think we need to practice our fighting?"

"Why?" I asked. "Artemis said our weapons would always work for us."

"I know that," Levi said. "But still, we don't actually know how to fight, do we?"

"You do," Frankie said. "You're always fighting with other kids at school."

"That's different," Levi said hotly. "That's normal fistfights. And I'm not always fighting!"

"You are," I corrected him. "You have at least three fights a day."

"I do not!" Levi shot back. "I just get angry at people."

"So do we," Frankie said stubbornly. "But we don't go round punching them in the face!"

"I don't mean to punch them!" Levi said, getting angry. "I just…"

"Just what?" I said. In the year I had been in the same class as Levi, I'd always imagined that he enjoyed being a bully. But after the last few days, I was starting to think that I might've been wrong.

"I just get angry," Levi said slowly. "At people. At nothing sometimes. And no one ever bothers to ask me why I get angry, do they? They just write me off as a troublemaker and a nuisance."

"You can be a bit of a nuisance," Frankie said.

"Well at least I don't think I'm better than everyone else!" Levi said angrily.

"I do not think that!" Frankie argued back.

"Yeah right!" Levi barked. "Just because your Dad's a lawyer, and your sister's dating the guy all the girls go mad for, you think it means you can judge everyone else!"

"I do not judge people!" Frankie said. "Do I Seb?"

"Of course he's going to say you don't!" Levi shouted. "He's your best friend, he's not going to tell you the truth is he?"

"Oi!" I said, shoving Levi. "Just because you can't handle—"

"What was that?" said Levi, changing the subject.

"What was what?" I asked. "And don't try to change the subject! We're having a row here!"

"Listen!" Levi growled. I didn't want to listen. Truth be told, I wanted to swing for him. I don't know why he was being so moody all of a sudden. It'd really felt like we'd gotten to see a different side to him since we'd met the gods. He wasn't the bully I thought he was, but he still liked an argument.

CRACK!

I leapt back. From under the ground, what looked like a massive buffalo with shaggy black fur had launched itself forward.

"What the hell is that thing?" Frankie screamed, making to

grab Peto. As Levi and I scrabbled for our swords, Frankie loosed an arrow, but as soon as the monster looked at it, it turned to stone.

"That can't be good!" I yelled, making sure to keep a good distance between me and the buffalo-monster, which had just let out a roar. Beachgoers ran in every direction, screaming.

I wished I could've joined them.

From behind me, Frankie loosed another volley of arrows, but as soon as the monster caught sight of them, they turned to stone and crumbled as soon as they hit the sand. I tried to run forward with my sword ready, but Levi pulled me back.

"Get off me!" I yelled, kicking out at him, but he still clung on to me.

"Look at the arrows!" Levi said, still pulling me away. "As soon as it looked at them they turned to stone!"

"So what?" I yelled, fighting against him. I was too ready for a fight to think clearly.

"If that thing catches sight of you, it'll be bye-bye Seb and hello Mr Statue!" Levi panted, still trying to keep me away from the monster.

"Seb, don't look at it!" Frankie ordered, joining Levi in pulling me back from the beast. She pulled out her sword, and Levi and I did the same thing. We crouched down low, keeping our eyes on the back of our shields and the sand around the monster.

"How are we going to fight it if we can't look at it?" I yelled. The monster was rearing itself up, kicking back against the sand, just waiting to charge at us.

"What do we do?" I yelled, trying desperately to think of some way of attacking the monster.

"I don't know!" Levi yelled back. The sound of sirens began

to echo from the distance. The last thing we needed was the police turning up and being faced with a monster that turned people to stone!

"Group prayer!" Frankie said suddenly, grabbing mine and Levi's arms.

"I know we're about to die," Levi yelled, as we leapt away from the monster together, still keeping our shields in front of us, "but why do we need to pray?"

"Not a prayer like that!" Frankie said, shoving me aside as the monster charged. We broke apart, keeping our shields up. "A prayer like the Greeks used to do! A prayer to the gods!"

"Which one?" Levi screamed, as the monster reared up, trying to get us to look at it.

"Artemis!" I thought out loud, before realising I had no idea what to say. "Um…"

Levi gritted his teeth, ready to leap aside as the monster reared up again. "Artemis, if you're hearing this, we could really use some help!"

Nothing happened. The monster still advanced, and we still backed away behind our shields.

No help was coming. For the third time since I met the gods, I was preparing to die. I got ready to jump as the monster panted and prepared to run at us.

"Archers! On my mark!"

I dared to hope that just maybe I wasn't hearing things, and Artemis really had come to help.

"You three!" the new voice barked. "Eyes down and back away from the Catoblepas!"

The three of us started moving away slowly. We heard volley after volley of arrows being loosed, until eventually the Catoblepas gave an almighty roar and then fell silent. A scream of fury echoed from somewhere nearby, loud and closer than I would have liked it to be.

"You may look up now," said the woman who had saved us. Her voice was different to Artemis, older, and with a distinct accent. I couldn't place it at first. It was like someone had taken Greek and mixed it up with something else.

"You're not Artemis," I said, cringing as I said it. No 'thanks for saving us' or 'that was awesome!'

I just told her she wasn't Artemis.

"Indeed, young man, I am not the Goddess," she said with a smile. She was dressed in immaculate golden armour, with a warrior's helm that covered most of her face. As she pulled it off, I took in her appearance. She looked middle-aged, maybe fifty? Fifty-five? She had long brown hair with a few streaks of grey, skin the colour of a perfect tan and shining blue eyes.

"My name is Otrera. I am Queen of the Amazons."

Chapter Twenty-Three
Frankie

You'd think, after the last few days, I'd have gotten used to meeting gods and heroes right?

But somehow, meeting Otrera was too much. I just stood there open-mouthed like a moron as she introduced us to her tribe of Amazon warriors. All women, all beautiful and all carrying enough weapons to defeat a small army.

"Tell me," Otrera said to Levi and Seb, "does your companion always look like that?"

"Like what?" Seb said defensively.

"An oversized goldfish," said Otrera. She didn't sound like she was trying to be cruel. She sounded genuinely concerned.

"Just... shocked," I said, finally remembering how to talk. "You're really the Amazons!"

"We are," said Otrera kindly. "And who are you? What gods are you champions for?"

"We're not champions," Levi said. "We're just normal kids."

"Mortals?" Otrera said in disbelief.

We nodded, and her eyes grew even wider.

"But...this is..." she grasped for the right words. "What are three mortal teenagers doing fighting the Catoblepas? And what are you doing near the Cave of Erebus?"

"The Cave of who?" Levi asked, shooting us a look. Where had we heard about Erebus before?

"Erebus," said Otrera. "The Lord of Darkness."

When the three of us looked at her blankly, Otrera sighed.

"Come," she said. "And I shall explain it all to you."

We followed her towards the far side of the beach, past the still-smoking ground where the Catoblepas had been ready to fight us.

"Hippolyta!" Otrera called, coming to a stop just beyond the smoking ground. A young girl of about our age came forward. "My daughter, bring us some chairs. And some food!" Otrera commanded. Hippolyta smiled at Levi as she brushed her long red hair out of her face. Levi looked as though he'd been hit over the head. Otrera coughed gently, and Levi blinked. He tried not to meet Hippolyta's eyes when she came back with the chairs. Behind her, some more of the Amazons appeared with plates of steaming food and goblets of drink.

"Eat and drink to your fill, children," Otrera smiled. "Let it not be said that the Amazons are not hospitable!"

"I thought," said Seb in between mouthfuls of what looked like Cherry Coke, "the Amazons hated boys?"

"Nonsense!" laughed Otrera. "We do not allow men to join our cause, that is true, and no Amazon can every marry," (Levi looked disappointed at that), "but we do not hate men! We're just... well, we just know we're better than them!"

I burst out laughing as Levi and Seb choked on their food. Otrera was fighting back a smile too.

"You can't actually think that!" Levi said, hotly.

"Of course I can," Otrera smiled. "I've had millennia to think about it. It is why I only allow women into my army. But let us not debate over the politics of my army. I believe it is time you heard the story of Erebus," she said, suddenly serious.

"Mother!" Hippolyta said quickly. "Is that wise?"

"Trust me, daughter. These mortals bear the protection of the gods. If they are getting mixed up in the gods' plans, it is only

173

right that they know who they are dealing with. Besides, Lady Artemis would not have sent us to them if she didn't think they deserved the truth."

"Artemis sent you?" I said, still tucking into the food the Amazons had provided.

"Of course, child. You prayed to her, did you not?" Otrera said.

"Well, yeah, but we didn't think she'd answer!" I said.

"Lady Artemis always comes to the aid of those who ask," said Otrera, nodding wisely. I guessed she'd had first-hand experience of Artemis answering her prayers.

"So, Erebus," Levi said. "He's the Primordial Deity of Darkness, right? The guy the Olympians were at war with?"

"It was bigger than that, young man," said Otrera quietly. "Much bigger. The War in Olympus affected everyone you have heard of from the myths. Some civilizations did not even make it past the first fight."

"But surely we'd know about it!" Seb put in. "If civilizations were missing, there'd be news reports! It should've gone viral by now!"

"I have no idea what viral means," said Otrera drily. "But time moves different on Olympus. Let us say the War in Olympus lasted only a matter of months. On Earth, going by your time, it lasted over a thousand years."

"How is that possible?" I said, trying to make sense of it.

"Only Aion, Titan of Eternity can answer that question," said Otrera. "If you think about the myths, I am sure you will work out which civilization I am referring to."

"Atlantis!" Seb shouted triumphantly.

"Precisely," said Otrera, sounding impressed. "Atlantis was the first of many civilizations to fall at the Primordial Deities' hands."

"But... why?" I said. "The Atlanteans hadn't done anything to the Primordial Deities!"

"Oh, but they had," said Otrera sadly. "What do you know of Atlantis?"

"It was an underwater city," said Levi, still with his eyes on Hippolyta.

"No, it wasn't," said Otrera. "It was an island. An island full of good, kind people who worshipped the gods. And that is what they did wrong. The war for Olympus had been raging for many years at this point. People's beliefs in the Primordial Deities had been failing. Many people who had once held the likes of Erebus and Aion, had long since abandoned that belief for belief in the gods. It was so on Atlantis. They had forsaken their temples to Pontus in favour of praying to Poseidon. At Erebus' command, Thanatos came to visit them. He was – and still is – Erebus' most feared lieutenant. He gave the Atlanteans a choice. Return to worshiping the Primordial Deities, and Thanatos would himself ensure they came to no harm in the war. When the Atlanteans refused his offer, he returned to Tartarus and told Erebus of it."

Otrera looked sad as she told the next part of Atlantis' history. "Erebus was enraged. Some say his rage rivalled that of even Ares, the god of War. He summoned Pontus, and instructed him to deal with the Atlanteans. Pontus had, you understand, been the Primordial Deity of the Sea, and there were some corners of the waters who were still loyal to him. He made sure that if the Atlanteans would not worship the Primordial Deities, they would not worship anyone."

"But couldn't the gods save them?" I asked, trying not to think of all those people Pontus had destroyed.

"It was too late. By the time word had reached Olympus of

Pontus' actions, Atlantis had already been sunk. There were, I'm sorry to say, no survivors."

"That's horrible!" said Seb.

"I know," said Otrera softly. "Those are the kinds of beings you are now dealing with, children. This War is not over. If you succeed in finding Lord Zeus he will want to claim Olympus as his once more. You must think very carefully about your next move."

"Which is what?" asked Levi.

"If you choose to help the gods further, you will open yourselves up to the fury of the Primordial Deities, and your fates will be sealed."

"And if we choose not to?" I asked quietly.

"Me and my warriors will take you back home to your families and wipe your memories of all the events that have happened in the last few days. You will lead perfectly normal lives, without the fear of retribution from the Primordial Deities."

The three of us looked at each other. If the Primordial Deities could sink an entire civilisation simply for refusing to worship them, what would they do to us for helping find Zeus?

"The prophecy," Seb whispered. "Remember what it said?"

I would never forget it for the rest of my life.

Lost to the winds in years gone by
The hunt must begin once more for the Lord of the Sky
Found not by Olympians, hidden away
Three mortals will find him or be tempted astray
Trapped in the concealed rock of grief
Death himself they must defeat.

I went over the prophecy in my head. *Lost to the winds in years gone by*. I had no idea how Zeus could have been lost to the winds, but I hoped he'd tell us when we found him. *The hunt must begin once more for the Lord of the Sky*. Well, that had

176

happened. It was what we were doing on this beach, surrounded by Amazonian warriors. *Found not by Olympians, hidden away.* The Olympians had been searching for Zeus for years, but they hadn't found him. *Three mortals will find him or be tempted astray.* I looked at Otrera. That line had to be about her. Here she was, giving us a golden opportunity to abandon the quest and go back home. I thought about the line that followed. *Trapped in the concealed rock of grief.* Everyone kept saying Zeus was hidden in the rock of grief, and if Pegasus had dropped us in the right place, we were close by. If we could just find out where it was!

I didn't allow myself to think about the next line.

"Have you made a decision?" asked Otrera gently.

The three of us locked eyes and nodded. We'd made our mind up.

"Queen Otrera," I said, going down to one knee before her. "Thank you for your most generous offer. But we have accepted a quest on behalf of the gods, and we intend to see it through."

Otrera smiled. "I thought you would say that. Will you accept a parting gift from us?"

We nodded our agreement. Hippolyta came forward and handed us each what looked like small lighters.

"These act as beacons," Otrera explained. "Light them and the Amazons will come to your aid. You must use them well, as they only work once."

We looked at them. Carved into the holder were images of the Amazons in battle, fierce warrior women in their element.

"Good luck," said Otrera, rising to her feet. "I hope you never have to use the beacons."

She bowed to each of us, and clapped her hands together.

"My women!" she called. "It is time we departed. Gather up your weapons. We must re-join our sisters back on Themiscyra."

The Amazons set about collecting up their belongings when all of a sudden there was a blinding flash of light. I heard the screams of the Amazons, and Otrera shouted out, in her clear voice, "Attack formation twenty! Stand your ground!"

I rubbed at my eyes, trying to get them to focus. I couldn't see what had happened, but the Amazons all had their weapons raised, and Otrera was leading them forward. Levi rushed over, tossing me my bow.

"Where's Seb?" I called. Levi looked grave. Where Seb had been stood was now a smoking pile of ash and burnt sand. I tried not to stare at the smoke.

I kept telling myself he was okay. We'd survived encounters with monsters and Tartarus. He was okay.

I hoped he was okay.

Chapter Twenty-Four
Seb

I hit the ground with a thump. It wasn't sand I landed on though. The ground was rough and hard, and wherever I was smelled of damp. I struggled to my feet, trying to focus on what was in front of me, and not the dizziness I was feeling. Wherever I was, it certainly wasn't the beach.

"Where... where am I?" I asked.

The walls were thick with dirt, and the only light was coming from a barred window high above us. I felt my legs go weak, and stumbled forward. I hadn't even noticed there was another man in the room with me until he caught me.

"Easy now!" he said gently. "Don't try to move too quickly."

"Where..." I mumbled. I couldn't think straight, my mind swimming with the images of the Amazons, and the sound of Queen Otrera's offer to take us back home.

"You'll be all right in a minute," the man said. He had broad shoulders and strong arms, and his grey hair was long. His face – the part of it that wasn't hidden by his shaggy grey beard – was kind, and his green eyes seemed to be giving off electrical sparks. "Do you know how you got here?" he asked gently, still supporting me as I tried to stand.

"We were on the beach..." I said, trying to remember. "We were looking for Zeus..."

"Zeus?" said the man, curiously. "Why were you looking for Zeus?"

"Quest," I managed to mumble. "Gods need him... trouble

179

with Thanatos…"

"That is not good," said the man. "Not good at all."

"Useless," I said. "Couldn't even find him. Just found the beach…"

"Oh, I think you did more than that," said the man. "Tell me, what is your name?"

"Seb," I answered. "Seb Morgan."

"Well, Seb Morgan, allow me to introduce myself. I am Zeus, Lord of the Sky."

We'd found him! If I hadn't been so fried by being blasted into the ground, I would've punched the air with delight. I looked up, and I knew at once that he was telling the truth. We'd found Zeus!

"But…" I began. Zeus smiled at me.

"Come. Sit with me and I shall explain where I have been," he said gently, leading me to what I now saw was a narrow bench. I sat down, my mind racing. I hadn't even noticed that Zeus had old-fashioned shackles around his legs. As he led me to the bench I saw him shuffling, like every movement he made caused him pain. As soon as we were sat down, two thick iron shackles wound their way around his wrists.

"Blasted things!" he roared. "Makes it near impossible to do anything here!"

I looked around and saw that not far ahead of me were another set of shackles, broken and cracked. I guessed Zeus must have broken them when I arrived.

"First, let me apologise for the rather theatrical way I brought you here," he said.

"That was you?" I asked, groggily.

"Indeed. I received your prayer to Artemis and sought to intervene. I trust I wasn't too late?"

"She already responded," I said, rubbing my throbbing head. "Sent the Amazons."

"Ah," said Zeus. "I had hoped to get you and your friends out of the way before they arrived. Wonderful people, the Amazons, but rather fond of violence. Unfortunately, I only had the power to bring you down here."

"But if you have power, why don't you just leave?" I asked confusedly.

"I cannot. Thanatos ensured when he imprisoned me that most of my power would be depleted. I have enough power to perform small acts, like bringing you here, but not enough to free myself."

I nodded. "I still don't understand how you got trapped down here," I said.

Zeus smiled. "Allow me to explain," he said.

"Many years ago, we received word from Olympus," Zeus said, conjuring an image before him. I saw a younger Zeus, his beard black instead of the grey it now was. "It was the first contact we had had with Olympus since Erebus' takeover."

The image showed a small glimmer of light, like a flame, flickering in front of Zeus's face.

"It was from Hestia, Goddess of the Hearth," Zeus continued, the image changing to show a white-haired old lady crouched in front of a barely burning fire. "She had stayed behind on Olympus to ensure the fire in the hearth never went out. As long as that fire burns, the heart of Olympus still exists."

"Lord Zeus, if you can hear me, you must act!" the image of Hestia was saying urgently. "You must find the Rock of Grief! Only by finding it will you be able to ensure your return to Olympus! Erebus is not as strong as he would have you believe, Majesty! He grows weaker by the day! He relies upon Thanatos and Tartarus to keep order on Olympus! Go to the Rock, Lord Zeus! Find the Rock and the sorrowful maiden and you will find a way back to Olympus!"

"The Sorrowful Maiden?" I asked, as the image changed again, back to the younger Zeus. He was clad in his bright gold battle armour, a massive helm covering his face, a lightning bolt in his hand.

"Indeed, the Sorrowful Maiden," said Zeus. "Allow me to explain. Many, many years ago, there lived a man named Creon. He was King of Thebes, a noble city. There had been a violent war, and two brothers had been killed. Creon demanded that one of the brothers, Polynices, not be buried," Zeus explained. I couldn't see what this had to do with why he was in the cave, but I didn't interrupt. "The problem was, Polynices' sister, a brave young woman named Antigone, defied this command. As a result, Creon had her buried alive in a cave."

"That's a normal response," I mumbled. Zeus laughed. "Antigone was a good woman, and, like most heroes and heroines of their tale, lives on. In this cave."

I blinked. Zeus was staring at a spot on the other side of the wall. "Is she here?" I asked, looking around.

"Oh yes." Zeus nodded. "Antigone is in this cave. This is the cave that became known as the Rock of Grief. It was so called because when Antigone was sealed up inside it, even us gods grieved for her. She had, you must understand, committed no crime except for loving her brother. Over time, this cave became one of the last places of power for Pontus, the Primordial Deity of the Sea."

"We've heard of him," I said. "He's the one who destroyed Atlantis."

"The very same," Zeus said. "When I set out twenty years

ago, I was coming to this cave," he explained. "Creon had ensured, you see, that no mortal would ever look upon Antigone again, but he did not put any obstacles up to stop the gods from visiting her. We all visited Antigone from time to time."

"So what happened?" I asked. I still couldn't see anyone else in the cave, but when Zeus spoke, he was talking to the same spot on the opposite wall.

"I arrived, as I always did, on the beach. To mortal beachgoers, Antigone's cave looks like it has eroded away to nothing. But to immortals, it is easily recognisable. The sealed up mouth of the cave is located only a few steps away from where the tide comes in. To access Antigone's prison, I must descend below the sea level. I had undertaken this journey many times before, and was expecting to see my dear friend waiting for me, perhaps with her brazier burning and a new story to tell me. But it was not Antigone who was waiting for me when I arrived, soaking wet and in need of a warm cup of tea."

The image in front of us changed again, now showing Zeus making his way into the cave. The woman who was waiting for him was young, with flowing brown hair and pale skin. She was wearing rags, but she was smiling as Zeus approached. As he embraced her, her figure began to flicker and change until, instead of Antigone, the hulking Pontus was stood in front of Zeus.

"As you can see," Zeus said. "I came face to face with Pontus."

The image changed again, this time showing Zeus fighting against Pontus, who was summoning water spirits and sharks and every kind of monster you can think of in an attempt to beat Zeus, who was throwing lightning bolts and blasting Pontus' monsters apart.

"It was a viscous fight," Zeus said sadly. "I had always known Pontus was lurking near the seabed, but I had hoped, when the day we met came, we could bargain. I would have allowed Pontus to control part of the seas if he swore to obey Olympus' rule. Unfortunately, he was in no mood for bargaining. That fight lasted for two whole weeks. It caused so much damage to the sea that I think Poseidon shall never forgive me for it."

"What happened?" I asked, trying not to look at the image in front of me, which was now showing Zeus ripping monsters apart with his bare hands.

"Pontus called for reinforcements. He summoned three of the worst Primordial Deities. Thanatos, Tartarus and Thalassa,"

"Are all the worst Primordial Deities the ones whose names begin with T?" I grinned, but Zeus looked so solemn I felt stupid for joking.

"Do not make light of it, Seb," he said. "Those three contained powers that even I could not best on my own. Thanatos is—"

"The Deity of Death, I know," I said, shuddering. I tried not to think of Clara, and whether he had let her go yet or whether she would be stuck with him inside her head for the rest of her life.

"Tartarus was the guardian of the worst and most hellish pit of the Underworld, which also bore his name. Thalassa was the Deity of the Sea. She ruled with Pontus and could match him in her power. The four of them together were unstoppable. It was no wonder they defeated me."

"But they didn't kill you?" I asked.

"Gods and their kind cannot be killed, Seb," Zeus said. "We can be injured, and our bodies can be stripped away, leaving us just as consciousness, but killed? Never."

"So what happened? And where was Antigone?"

"They imprisoned me here," Zeus said bitterly. "They had upgraded Antigone's cave in secret. The boulders that Creon used to block her in have been replaced with layers of Stygian steel. It is unbreakable and inescapable." Zeus seemed like he was thinking hard about what he said next. "You asked about Antigone's whereabouts. There is a curse placed on this cave. When Thanatos discovered that Antigone had been receiving visitors, he cursed the cave to only hold two people at any one time. It means Antigone can never see more than one of the gods at one time."

"That doesn't sound so bad," I said, but Zeus shook his head.

"Ah, but it is. You see, Antigone is regarded highly by the gods. Some of them – I shall not say who – prize the ability to visit her more than others. They see it as a mark of their power, that they are so easily able to defy the demands of a mortal. The fact that Thanatos had restricted that power led to countless rows between the gods as to who should visit Antigone the most often."

"That's so childish!" I said. Zeus laughed.

"It is, I agree. But my family are not very good at rational discussion. The arguments drove an ever greater wedge between some of my children."

"You said the cave had been blocked up by Stygian steel," I said. "That's the steel made from the Styx isn't it?"

"It is," said Zeus. "Forged by Styx herself. If a prison is constructed from it, it means no immortal being may enter or leave without the jailer unlocking the doors. Hence why me and my friends have been stuck here for so long."

"You and your friends?" I said. As far as I could see, it was only Zeus in the cave with me.

"My dear boy, look around you," Zeus said. "Can't you see them?"

"It's just dark," I said plainly. "That's all."

"Ah, mortals. It's been so long since I was around them," Zeus sighed. "I forgot that your eyesight's are terrible."

"Hey!" I protested. "I have twenty-twenty vision, thank you!"

"Compared to us gods, your eyesight is awful," Zeus chuckled. "Cover your eyes."

I did as he said. There was an almighty shout, and what sounded like a million little explosions. When I opened my eyes again, the room was bathed in a bright blue light, and we were not the only two people in the room.

"Seb," Zeus smiled. "Meet the Constellation Council."

Imagine the strangest collection of creatures you can. Imagining it? Now multiply that by about a million and you've got the Constellation Council. There were at least forty different creatures, and each of them were chained to the wall.

"These are the beings that make the rules for what immortals can do on Earth," Zeus explained. I was still stood open mouthed, starting at the Council.

"It is rude to stare!" snapped the Council member closest to me. He was a bright red fox, with a bushy tail and beady eyes.

"Forgive him, Vulpecula," said Zeus. "It is his first time seeing you all."

Vulpecula grumbled something about 'ignorant mortals' but otherwise didn't say another word.

"You're the Constellations?" I asked. "As in, the constellations in the sky?"

"Sort of," smiled a woman who was chained up next to Vulpecula. "I'm Andromeda," she said. "I would shake your

186

hands, but the chains make it a bit difficult. The Constellations are representations of us, created by the Gods to denote our position within Olympus."

That didn't make it any clearer, but I nodded anyway.

"How come you're all chained up here?" I asked. The Constellation Council laughed in response, but Andromeda smiled.

"We attempted to come to Zeus' aid when Pontus summoned his reinforcements," she explained. "But he knew we were coming. He'd prepared defences to make sure we could not help Zeus. He imprisoned us as soon as we arrived."

I looked around. Something wasn't adding up. How had Pontus, who had struggled to defeat Zeus been able to capture every member of the Constellation Council?

"We don't know," Andromeda said. I realised with a jolt that she had read my thoughts.

"Will everyone stop reading my thoughts!" I growled.

Most of the Council mumbled apologies.

"We've always suspected that someone told Pontus we were coming," Vulpecula said quietly.

"A spy?" I asked. Vulpecula nodded.

"We've never been able to prove it, but that's the only way Pontus could have known we were coming and trapped us in here."

I thought back to when Artemis had packed us off on this quest. It had only been three days, but it felt like a lifetime. She had asked us to try and find the Constellations. I guess we'd found them after all.

"Wait!" I said quickly, an idea forming in my head. "If there was a spy, why didn't Pontus spare them?"

"Olympus only knows," said another of the Council. This

man had more muscles than I'd ever thought possible and intense green eyes.

"Hercules?" I murmured.

"Herakles," he corrected me. "We never knew if it was one of us, or if Pontus had sent another Primordial Deity to spy on us. Whatever way he found out, it worked. He had us bound to the wall in chains before any of us had a chance to react. We've been stuck here with Lord Zeus ever since."

"But why trap you all here?" I asked. "Couldn't they have sent you to Tartarus?"

"They would not dare!" said the man next to Herakles. "They would never send me to the place I sent Medusa!"

"You beheaded Medusa?" I repeated, wracking my brain to remember who it was that had faced the Gorgon.

"I did. I am Perseus," he said with a small smile. "I took on a Gorgon, and look where it got me. Imprisoned with these creatures!"

"Creatures!" roared Vulpecula. "Did you just call us creatures?"

There were mingled shouts of indignation from all around, and it looked like any minute now the Council would break their bonds and start fighting each other.

"BE QUIET!" Zeus yelled. Every member of the Council instantly fell silent. I could see the electrical sparks firing off in his eyes. "After over a thousand years, you still cannot get along!"

"He called us creatures!" Vulpecula complained. "He's the one who beheaded a woman, and he calls us creatures!"

"I did a service for the Olympians, sending that thing to Tartarus! What have you ever done?"

"ENOUGH!" Zeus growled. From somewhere far overhead,

188

a great rumble of thunder echoed. "I will not tolerate this any longer!"

I coughed quietly. Every pair of eyes turned to stare at me.

"Can I ask," I said, staring at the floor. "If Tartarus is the only one who can get you out, why didn't you try and take control of him and make him do it?"

"We cannot do that," Andromeda said. "It would be improper. Only an immortal with no morals would do such a thing!"

"Thanatos has done it," I said. "He's taken over my friend."

"What?" squawked another member of the council, who looked like an oversized raven.

"I said, Thanatos has taken over my friend," I said.

"Do try to pay attention Corvus," Zeus said. "I am aware of Miss Liu's current predicament. I had a visit from her not long before your arrival."

"Can you help her?" I asked. Zeus nodded.

"I can, and I will once I am free."

"Impossible!" growled a bear that was chained near Zeus. "Once an immortal has control of a mortal it cannot be undone!"

"That would usually be correct, Ursa Major – Minor, stop snapping at him – it should be completely impossible. But you forget, you are talking to me. When have I ever allowed a small thing such as possibility get in the way of doing something?"

"How will you do it?" the smaller bear said.

"I do not know, Ursa Minor. But I shall think of something. I will not see another mortal suffer at Thanatos' hands."

That got a reaction from the Council. There were mutters and titters, and Zeus looked satisfied with himself.

"We must try and think of a way out of here," he said. "Seb, do you have any ideas?"

189

"Me?" I said. "I don't even know how I ended up down here, Zeus. One minute I was on the beach, the next I was flat on my face. I can't help you."

From somewhere outside the cave I heard the jangling of keys and smelt smoke.

"Tartarus!" Andromeda said. "He approaches!"

"What will we do?" Corvus squawked.

"Ambush him!" Perseus said hotly. "Steal the keys from him and send him into his own pit!"

"In case you've forgotten," Herakles muttered, "we're chained to the wall! We can't ambush anyone!"

"I can," I said quietly. "I'm not chained up, am I?"

"No," said Zeus. "I will not allow it. Tartarus is dangerous. You don't know what he is capable of."

"We fought him," I said confidently. "Back at your old house in Edinburgh. And we won."

"You won," said Zeus. "Because Pegasus summoned Hades to defend you. Seb, your intentions are noble, but if you fight Tartarus, you'll be doing it on your own. No help from any of us."

"I've got a sword," I said, pulling Ekfitos out and showing to Zeus.

"Where did you get that?" Andromeda asked, staring at it.

"From Artemis. She gave us all weapons and armour before we left Asfaleia House."

"What have I told you about allowing your daughter to hand out weapons?" Vulpecula snarled at Zeus.

"Vulpecula, I do not know what you have told me," Zeus said. "I hardly listen when you talk."

The council looked like they were about to start arguing again, but Andromeda put a stop to it.

190

"Do none of you realise what this means?" she said. "Seb, that sword is made of Stygian steel! It can cut through the chains that Tartarus has bound us in!"

Tartarus was getting closer to our cell, so I had to act fast.

"Do it, mortal! Cut the chains that bind us!" Vulpecula snapped.

"You must free us!" Ursa Major roared. "Quickly, before Tartarus arrives!"

"Major, don't roar at the poor boy!" Andromeda scolded him. "Seb, when you are ready, all you have to do is make sure your sword connects with each of the chains. That's it. Nothing more, nothing less."

Zeus was leaning forward, staring at Ekfitos. The iron shackles that held him in place were straining to keep him tied up.

"That sword..." he said.

"Do you recognise it, Lord Zeus?" asked Herakles.

"I do," Zeus confirmed. "It was forged by Hephaestus, during the war. I used it myself in close combat with Erebus. It was near unstoppable."

"That's good though, isn't it?" I asked. It hadn't felt near-unstoppable when I'd been fighting against Tartarus.

"It can be," Zeus said. "As long as it is in the right hands. If a Primordial Deity got their hands on it..."

"They won't," I said automatically. I almost believed it. Zeus looked satisfied, and edged closer to me, holding his wrists out.

"Try and cut the chains around my wrists," Zeus instructed, with a reassuring smile.

I breathed in. If Zeus was wrong, I'd hear a clang and my sword might shatter. I raised the sword, and brought it down on the chains—

They fell away as if they were made of water.

"THANK OLYMPUS!" Zeus beamed. "Now the ones around my legs!"

I did the same for the chains around Zeus' legs, and they fell away. The King of the Gods gave a shout and jumped up in delight.

"At last!" he cheered. "Now do the others!"

After hacking and slashing my way through all the other chains, I eventually freed the Constellation Council.

"Now all we need to do is work out how to get out of here," Andromeda said.

As if on cue, the sound of Tartarus' footsteps stopped right outside the cave. The wall gave a shudder and began to fall away.

"Quickly!" Zeus whispered. "Get back against the wall! We have to surprise him!"

We all did as he said, pressing ourselves tightly back against the wall. The wall gave one final shudder and crumbled away to nothing, and Tartarus, his suit smoking, and his body looking like he'd aged about a hundred years since I last saw him, walked into the cell.

"Show yourself!" he demanded.

"I am here," Zeus said, leaning out of the shadows. "Where you and Thanatos have ensured I remain."

"Good," snarled Tartarus. "You will die here, Zeus. I shall see to it that your mortal saviours are blasted apart. And then, Lord Erebus will reward me for my service! I shall sit in the throne that once belonged to your wife, Hera. I shall command an entire legion of monsters! I shall—"

THUMP

Tartarus hit the ground. Herakles stood over him, his knuckle red.

192

"Do you ever stop talking?" he asked.

"What... how..." Tartarus stammered, clambering to his feet. As soon as he got up, Vulpecula leapt forward, pouncing on him.

"Get off me!" Tartarus roared. "Foul creature!"

"How dare you!" Vulpecula snapped, his teeth dangerously close to Tartarus' neck. From underneath him, Tartarus snarled like a wild animal. He shoved at Vulpecula, who lost his balance and rolled off of his captive. Tartarus leapt to his feet.

"What is this?" he demanded.

"This," said Zeus calmly. "Is what I believe the mortals call a jailbreak."

Several things happened at once. Zeus launched himself at Tartarus, and sent him sprawling backwards. As he fell, Vulpecula darted towards him and snapped up the keys to cave. Ursa Major and Ursa Minor caught Tartarus between them and began to run with him towards the entrance. Zeus grinned at me as we chased after them, Herakles ahead of us with Perseus and Andromeda. Overhead, Corvus was swooping in and out of our lines of vision, keeping his eyes on Tartarus. We came to a stop at the mouth of the cave, where Ursa Major and Minor were taking in turns to shove Tartarus against the Stygian steel entrance bars. Vulpecula had inserted the keys into the lock, but nothing was happening.

"Why won't it open?" he demanded, snapping his teeth.

"You need my command," said Tartarus groggily. "I have to give the order."

"Then do so!" Herakles demanded. "Free us!"

"No," Tartarus breathed out. "I will be punished."

"You'll be punished either way," said Perseus. "Let us out, or we will send you to your own pit."

"Lord Erebus will do that if I let you out," Tartarus whimpered.

"Open. That. Door," Zeus said threateningly. "Or I will personally throw you down to your pit and ensure you never resurface."

Tartarus gave a whimper. Whatever he did, it was not going end well for him.

"Cave, open yourself," he whimpered. The Stygian steel fell away, and finally, the Constellation Council and Zeus were free. They tumbled out into the sunlight, carrying Tartarus with them, and began to rise up through the sea.

"Wait!" I said. "What about me?"

Herakles took my arm. Together we floated up, a bubble of air keeping us safe. We saw the Constellations ascended one by one back into the sky as we broke the surface. Andromeda waved at me, and I waved back as she flew up, Vulpecula snapping at her heels. Ursa Major and Minor were still holding onto Tartarus who dropped like a stone as they began to ascend. After a few minutes, it was just Zeus, Herakles and me stood over the spluttering Tartarus.

"I wish you good fortune," said Herakles, nodding to me. "Whatever decision you take in regards to Tartarus' punishment, I know it will be the right one."

He ascend on upwards, and disappeared in a flash of light. Tartarus was trying to stand up, but kept falling backwards onto the sand.

"What do we do with him?" I asked Zeus.

"I shall handle him," Zeus said darkly. He raised his hand, and the sand split under us, until a chasm just like the one Tartarus had opened up in Zeus' house was in front of me.

"You're sending him down to Tartarus?" I said.

"I am," said Zeus. Tartarus whimpered again.

"Please…" he mumbled. "Not there…"

"Why not?" Zeus snarled. "You conspired with the Winds to kidnap me! You aided Pontus and Thanatos in my capture! You have jailed me and the council for twenty years!"

"I was only following orders!" Tartarus whined. "I did not mean any harm!"

"You tried to kill the very people who were looking for me!"

"It was an order! I did not mean to cause harm! It was all Thanatos' doing! He made me—AHHHH!"

Tartarus toppled over and fell head first into the chasm, screaming all the way down. Zeus leapt back, pulling me with him.

"You sent him down there?" I said accusingly.

"I did no such thing!" Zeus said. "It wasn't me!"

The chasm sealed itself up. There was no one else here, so it had to have been Zeus.

"Over there!" Zeus said, spinning me around to look behind us. I saw Levi and Frankie, along with a band of fierce warrior women fighting against what looked like sea-spirits and the water itself.

"Is it Pontus?" I said, starting to run towards them.

"No," said Zeus, running alongside me. "I'm afraid it's your friend."

He was right. In the middle of the fight, a longsword drawn, was Clara.

And she was heading straight for Frankie and Levi.

Chapter Twenty-Five
Frankie

The lightning flash that had sent us sprawling backwards had also set the beach on fire. The Amazons were huddled together, their weapons drawn, as high above another blast of lightning rained down on the beach.

"Who's doing that?" I called. Levi and I had found ourselves huddled up with Hippolyta, who had drawn her sword, and was slowly moving forward.

"Look!" Hippolyta said coldly. "Up ahead!"

I raised my eyes and saw Clara stood in front of us. She was holding onto what looked like an unending supply of lightning bolts and was throwing them, one after the other at the Amazons.

"YOU HAVE INTERFERED IN MY PLANS ONE TOO MANY TIMES, OTRERA!" she called in the voice of Thanatos. "NOW YOU WILL SUFFER!"

"Take cover!" Otrera called. The Amazons lifted their shields, Hippolyta making sure hers covered Levi as I raised my own. The bolt blasted off of the shields and rebounded.

"Target hit!" Otrera called to us. "Do not lower your shields!"

On and on it went, until I felt like I couldn't take another hit from Clara. Hippolyta looked exhausted too, and I knew we were close to giving up.

"Why is she doing this?" Levi called, still crouched under Hippolyta's shield.

"I don't know," Hippolyta answered as another bolt glanced off our shields.

I chanced a glance at where Seb had been stood. The sand was still smoking, and I tried not to think about the possibility that he might have been sent to the Underworld.

"We have to attack!" Hippolyta called. "On my signal, break cover and charge."

"She'll kill us!" Levi said, panicked.

"It's our only chance!" Hippolyta said. "If we stay like this, she'll end up breaking our shields apart! Amazons, on my command!"

"No!" Otrera called back. "We stay in cover!"

"One..." Hippolyta began counting, ignoring her mother's command. "Two..."

"Hippolyta, you must not fight her!" Otrera called, desperate.

"CHARGE"! Hippolyta screamed. The Amazons broke into two groups, those who stayed with Otrera, and those who broke off with Hippolyta. Levi and I stayed frozen to the spot as Hippolyta and her group charged, rushing towards Clara, who tried to blast them apart.

The Amazons were ferocious fighters, charging at Clara with their weapons drawn.

"They're going to kill her!" I screamed, beginning to run after them. "Hippolyta, stop!"

"It's her or us!" Hippolyta called back viciously. Gone was the sweet girl who we had met earlier, replaced by an angry, battle-hardened warrior.

"She's our friend!" Levi called, catching up with us, dodging more bolts from Clara.

"Then you should have picked your friends more wisely!" Hippolyta screamed. Her group of Amazons had formed a circle around Clara, their weapons drawn.

"Queen Otrera, stop them!" I begged. The Queen of the Amazons looked torn, but took off with her group, launching an attack against Hippolyta's followers.

"Mother, what are you doing?" Hippolyta demanded, matching her mother's every stroke.

"Stopping you from killing a child!" Otrera bellowed, knocking Hippolyta's sword aside. Clara had stopped firing, taking in the scene around her. The Amazons were fighting against each other now, and Levi and me took our chance and rushed forward to Clara.

"Stay there!" she demanded, in her own voice. "He's not finished yet!"

"You've got to fight him!" I said. Clara's eyes were back to their normal colour now, but her voice was strained, as if she was trying to hold down a cough.

"I can't," she whispered. "He's too strong. It was him that summoned Tartarus... he won't stop until he's killed you."

Levi looked at me. We had to think of something. There had to be a way of getting Thanatos out of Clara's head.

With the Amazons still hacking at each other, with Clara trying desperately to keep Thanatos at bay, it seemed like we'd failed. I was prepared to give up, to let Thanatos win, when we heard a sound like a trumpet call, and out of nowhere Seb reappeared beside us.

"Where the hell have you been?" I shrieked, jumping on him.

"Mmmhmm," came his muffled response. I let go of him, and he said, "I found Zeus."

"You what?" Levi said, shocked.

"He said," said a new voice. "He found me."

I turned round. Besides Seb stood a man whose face I had only seen in the photos Artemis had given us. I gasped.

"Hello," smiled Zeus. "I am Zeus. And I'm here to deal with Thanatos."

Chapter Twenty-Six
Clara

I was trying so hard to fight against Thanatos. I could feel him in my head, screaming and shouting, louder than ever.

"KILL THEM! KILL THEM BOTH! DO IT NOW!"

I wanted to scream, or cry, or both. I wanted him out of my head. I wanted to go home, to sit with Mama and Baba and read stories about the Greek gods. I didn't want to be here. I didn't want to have to fight my friends.

"I SAID KILL THEM, YOU FOOLISH GIRL! DO IT!" Thanatos screamed again. "THEY ARE YOUR ENEMIES! YOU ARE A SERVANT OF EREBUS, AND YOU WILL DO AS HE COMMANDS!"

"No," I managed to croak. "No I won't."

I didn't have time to try and fight against Thanatos again, because at that moment, Zeus and Seb appeared.

"Zeus..." I managed to whisper. The King of the Gods looked at me and smiled. "Please..."

"Do not worry Clara," he said gently. "I will not harm you. I will, however, harm the being that thinks it is acceptable to use you as a hiding place."

"THAT IS A SHAME," I said in Thanatos' voice. "BECAUSE I AM GOING TO HURT YOU."

Chapter Twenty-Seven
Levi

Clara's words – Thanatos' words – rang out. Zeus looked at Clara and smiled.

"No, my dear, you are not going to hurt me. The being who has taken over your mind, he wants to hurt me, but you do not."

"I WILL SEE YOU IMPRISONED IN TARTARUS WITH THAT FAILURE OF A JAILER!" Thanatos spat.

"Ah," said Zeus. "So it was you who made him take that little tumble was it?"

"HE FAILED LORD EREBUS. HE DESERVED PUNISHMENT."

"I wonder," said Zeus. "What punishment will he have for you?"

"NONE," snarled Thanatos. "I WILL NOT FAIL HIM! SOON, THESE AMAZONIANS WILL TEAR EACH OTHER APART, AND WHEN THEY ARE FINSIHED, I WILL SET MY WRATH UPON YOU AND THESE MORTALS."

"Interesting plan," said Zeus. "It's not going to work though."

"WHY IS THAT?" Thanatos asked. Clara was stood facing Zeus, but every time he stepped towards her, she moved back, as if she was afraid of him.

"Well, for starters, you can't kill me, and these mortals carry the blessing of the gods. Regretfully, Clara does not carry the same. If she did, she would have been able to force you from her head much sooner."

"SHE WELCOMED ME," Thanatos crooned. "SHE GLADLY ACCEPTED HER DESTINY."

"It's a funny thing, destiny," said Zeus. "Don't you think?"

"Is this really the time for a philosophical debate?" I asked, diving out of the way to two Amazonians who were trying to rip each other's armour off.

"I think so," said Zeus, stepping out of Hippolyta's way as she darted past us. "You see, there was a prophecy about a girl who would either aid or hinder Erebus in his quest to keep me from Olympus."

"Never mind that!" said Frankie. "Now you're here, does that mean you can help get him out of Clara's head?"

"I believe I can," said Zeus. "But it is not my choice."

"What?" Seb said. "How can it not be your choice to help her?"

"You will understand soon," Zeus said. "But before I attempt to deal with Thanatos, I must deal with these Amazonians."

Zeus pulled a thunderbolt from the sky and tossed it to the ground. It flashed and a flame shot up into the air in brilliant blue. Overhead, an eagle screeched.

"That eagle was outside Asfaleia House!" Seb said, as it came to land on Zeus' shoulder.

"Indeed?" asked Zeus, raising his eyebrow.

"YOUR SACRED ANIMAL CANNOT HELP YOU NOW," Thanatos taunted.

"Be quiet," Zeus said. "I shall deal with you in a minute."

The Amazons had dropped their weapons and were kneeling on the burnt and blackened sand, their heads bowed.

"Finally!" Zeus said. "Have you quite finished your little dispute?"

"Lord Zeus," Otrera breathed out. "You have returned."

"Yes, thank you for pointing out the obvious," Zeus said. "I will deal with this ridiculous nonsense later, Otrera. For now, reunite and ready your women. We have a fight on our hands."

Otrera bowed low. The Amazons picked up their weapons and regrouped, standing as one behind us.

"As for you," Zeus said darkly, his eyes fixed on Clara, "I shall enjoy this."

He picked up another bolt and threw it with all his might at Clara.

"NO!" Frankie screamed, as Seb and I both let out yells of shock. The bolt smashed into Clara, sending her crumpling to the ground.

"You killed her!" Seb shouted. "You killed her!"

"Did I?" asked Zeus. I looked over to where Clara had fallen. She was lying flat on her back, her eyes closed. "Or did I begin the process to remove her unwelcome visitor?"

We looked at where Clara had been standing. The ground was smoking, and Thanatos, looking like he'd just boxed twelve rounds with Zeus, was stood beside Clara, clawing at the ground.

"Thanatos," Zeus growled. "You took over the mind of a child, and for what?"

"REVENGE," drawled Thanatos. "YOU HAVE ALWAYS LOVED YOUR CREATIONS. WHAT BETTER WAY TO GET OUR REVENGE ON YOU THAN BY USING ONE OF THEM TO KEEP YOU OUT OF OLYMPUS?"

"You swine!" Zeus scowled. "You willingly used the mind of a child to try and get revenge on me!"

Thanatos laughed that sick laugh. "SHE WELCOMED THE CHANCE TO SERVE MASTER EREBUS."

"Liar!" I shouted. "Clara would never help Erebus!"

"WHAT DO YOU KNOW?" Thanatos snapped at me.

"YOU KNOW NOTHING OF EREBUS, OF THE POWER HE IS WILLING TO GRANT HER! POWER TO MAKE PEOPLE SEE HER AS SHE IS!"

"You lured her in with promises of power?" Zeus said.

"SHE DID NOT NEED CONVINCING," Thanatos mocked. "SHE WAS PREPARED TO SERVE EREBUS."

"He's lying!" Frankie said. "There's no way Clara would ever serve someone like Erebus!"

"LET US ASK HER," Thanatos whispered, confidently. "SEE WHO SHE WILL CHOOSE."

Zeus looked uneasy. Clara was climbing to her feet.

"What... where am I?" she asked. Frankie and Seb were grinning at her.

"What do you remember?" I asked.

"There was a man... he said something about a prophecy..." Clara said.

"YOU ARE THE KEY TO KEEPING THE GODS AWAY!" Thanatos said. Clara screamed.

"It's him! He was at school! He's working with the old man we saw!"

"We know," I said. "He's..."

How could I tell her Thanatos had been inside her head? That he'd made her fight us?

"He has made use of your mind," Zeus said. "As unpleasant as it is, he has made you fight your friends."

"Did... did I hurt anyone?" Clara asked.

"Nah," said Seb.

"No one," said Frankie.

"I mean, I got a few scratches, but apart from that—" I grinned. Clara grinned back.

"DECIDE, CLARA LIU!" Thanatos shouted. "YOU MUST

STAND WITH EREBUS. YOU MUST WELCOME ME BACK INTO YOUR HEAD! TOGETHER WE WILL SERVE EREBUS AND RULE OVER CREATION! ALL YOUR WORRIES WILL DISAPPEAR! YOU WILL BE SEEN FOR WHAT YOU ARE! INTELLIGENCE SHALL BE YOURS! YOU WILL HAVE SERVANTS OF YOUR OWN! YOU DO NOT NEED THESE MORTALS!"

"What are you saying?" asked Clara, unsteadily.

"ALLOW ME BACK INTO YOUR MIND," Thanatos said. "AND WE SHALL RULE ALONGSIDE LORD EREBUS!"

"Clara," said Zeus. "The time has come for you to make a choice. You must decide whether to allow Erebus back into your mind or not."

"What happens if I refuse?" Clara asked, looking at Thanatos.

Zeus sucked in a breath. It looked like he was choosing his next words with care, like each one was a bomb that could go off at any second.

"The battle to reclaim Olympus will begin."

Chapter Twenty-Eight
Clara

If I agreed to let Thanatos back into my head, I could make sure the gods never got near Olympus again. I could rule alongside Erebus, with all the knowledge I could ever want. Every book I'd ever wanted to read, I could read. I could master every subject at school. I could make people realise I was more than just Clara, who was quiet and got good marks in her lessons.

"YOU KNOW WHICH TO CHOOSE," Thanatos said. He was right. I knew exactly which option I would choose. I looked at Seb, Frankie and Levi. They'd been through so much to try and find me. They'd found Zeus, and now the King of the Gods wanted me to say no to Thanatos. If I did, he'd told me the battle for Olympus would start. I didn't want to be responsible for starting a war. I just wanted my bed.

"YOU WILL HAVE SERVANTS TO WAIT UPON YOUR EVERY WHIM," Thanatos said. "THEY WILL DO WHATEVER YOU COMMAND."

I could make them do anything I wanted. I could command anyone to obey my every demand.

I looked at Thanatos. He looked weak, and in an instant I knew what I had to say.

"Thank you for freeing me, Lord Zeus," I said. "I have made my choice."

Zeus looked at me expectantly.

"I have had Thanatos in my head for the last few days," I said. "Not by my choice."

"YOU WELCOMED MY ARRIVAL!" Thanatos snarled.

"YOU WERE GLAD TO HAVE A PURPOSE! TO BE FREE OF YOUR MORTAL FRIENDS!"

"I have begged you to leave my head!" I shouted angrily. "How does that sound like I welcomed you?"

"YOU KNOW EREBUS WILL HAVE PLANS FOR YOU! YOU COULD RULE—"

"I don't want to rule!" I said. "I want a normal life! I want normal friends, and a normal family, and the chance to choose who I side with!"

Zeus was smiling at me. I wasn't finished with Thanatos yet.

"You stole my mind! You made me do things I would never have done. I want no part of your plans, or Erebus' plans, or anyone else's who thinks it's okay to steal my mind!"

"Go on Clara!" Levi whooped.

"YOU WILL SIDE WITH LORD EREBUS!" Thanatos snapped, starting to walk towards me. "OR YOU WILL DIE!"

I looked into the eyes of Death himself, and I wasn't scared. I watched as he pulled himself up to his full height and towered over me. I had no weapon, no way of defending myself against him. I didn't care. He was out of my head and I had made my choice. No matter what Thanatos or Erebus offered me, there was no chance of me ever siding with them. Thanatos raised his hand, and I could feel myself growing weaker by the second.

"I SHALL DRAIN YOUR LIFE FROM YOU," he said. "AND YOUR REMAINS SHALL BE USED AS A SACRIFICE TO EREBUS!"

I tried to move, but it felt like I was pushing through treacle. My legs were moving, but I wasn't getting away. I felt weak, like I could drop down and sleep for a hundred years. Thanatos was grinning. His plan to drain my life was obviously working.

"NOW!" shouted Zeus. The Amazonians let loose arrow after arrow, which all connected with Thanatos. As he stumbled back, Levi ran over to me and pulled me behind his shield. I felt instantly more alert than I had, and realised that the enchantment over me must have broken. I peeked over the top in time to see Seb and Frankie taking in turns to swipe at Thanatos, Frankie using her bow as a makeshift sword. Thanatos was giving as good as he got, brushing the Amazonian's arrows off of him with ease, and catching each of Seb and Frankie's blows. I picked up a discarded arrow and darted out from behind Levi's shield, plunging it deep into Thanatos' shoulder.

"ENOUGH OF THIS!" Thanatos screamed in frustration as ichor, the golden blood of the god, poured out of where I had plunged the arrow. "I WILL DESTROY YOU ALL."

"No," said Zeus darkly. "You will not. Cover your eyes!"

We all did as he said. The Amazonians dropped low on the sand, one hand over their eyes, while Seb and Frankie crouched down behind their shields. Levi pulled me down so our eyes were level with the back of his shield. There was a blinding flash of light, and Thanatos let out a horrific scream.

"You may look up now," said Zeus. When we got up, he was fixing his shirt, and where Thanatos had been stood was now just a smoking pile of ash which the wind was already carrying away.

"What did you do?" I asked.

"I assumed my true form," Zeus said, examining the particles that had been Thanatos. "If looked upon by mortals, or by those who have recently left the head of a mortal, it will incinerate them."

"He's dead?" I said, coming to kneel beside Zeus.

"Not dead," he said, running some Thanatos-ash through his fingers. "But I doubt he will bother you again."

"Thank you," I said, relieved. "I thought I'd never get rid of him."

"It was no bother," Zeus said breezily. "And you even fulfilled an old prophecy for me."

"I did?" I asked, standing up. I felt light-headed, but Zeus was gripping my arm to keep me upright.

"There was a prophecy that a mortal girl would decide whether Erebus was kept on Olympus, or whether the gods would make one final stand to win it back."

"And I decided the outcome?" I said confused.

"You did indeed. By not allowing Thanatos to return to your head and provide Erebus with an easy way to keep us down here, you have decided that the gods must make their final attempt at winning back at Olympus."

"I didn't mean to," I said in shock.

"Do not look so alarmed," Zeus said. "If you had agreed, Erebus would have been able to use you to keep us busy. We would have had been fighting you, and Thanatos in your head for years. But now that he's gone, we can start planning to retake our home. And, I, for one, cannot wait to kick Erebus off my throne."

"My Lord," Otrera said. "My women and I must return to Themyscria."

"Ah, yes," said Zeus, turning to face the Amazons. "I had almost forgotten about your little dispute. Hippolyta, come forth."

Hippolyta stepped forward, bowing her head low.

"Tell me," said Zeus. "What reason have you to doubt your mother's leadership?"

"None, my Lord," Hippolyta said sulkily.

"You must have some reason, if you willingly disobeyed her."

"She is too hot-headed, my Lord," said Otrera. "I shall see that she is punished. I should expel every single Amazon who disobeyed my command not to attack."

Hippolyta looked shame faced at me and mouthed the word sorry. There was a part of me that wanted to see her banished, but I knew she was only doing what she thought was right.

"Queen Otrera," I said. "I know what your daughter and her

followers did was wrong, but they did think it was for the best," Hippolyta shot me a smile. "So, maybe, you could… not expel them?"

Queen Otrera looked at me. "She is wise," she said loudly. "Clearly Metis has blessed her."

Zeus swatted at his head, as if there was an invisible fly buzzing around him. "Yes, I heard," he grumbled. "Now stop buzzing around! Take a piece of advice, children," he said, irritably. "Never take the form of a lizard and swallow your lover whose in the form of a fly!"

"Duly noted," smirked Levi.

"I have heard your counsel," said Queen Otrera, looking at me. "And I will heed your advice. I shall not expel my daughter and her followers."

There was a sigh of relief from Hippolyta. "But I shall think of a punishment worthy of the crime!" Queen Otrera added.

"We shall leave you to your decisions, Your Majesty," smiled Zeus. "I trust we shall cross paths again. Farewell!"

We all said our goodbyes before Zeus led us down the beach, and let out a low whistle. "Come to me!" he called. At once, there was a low-pitched whinny, and Pegasus, his white wings outstretched, kamikazed down to meet us.

"Big boss!" he called. "You're not dead!"

"Indeed I am not!" Zeus chuckled. "I have a job for you, old friend. We need to get to Asfaleia House, and quickly."

"Hop on!" called Pegasus. We all clambered on, and Pegasus let out a neigh as he began to ascend towards the sky.

"Oh, I have missed this!" roared Zeus. "Pegasus, do your trick!"

We all clung on for dear life as Pegasus, with a whoop, dived down to towards the sea, pulling up at the last minute.

Chapter Twenty-Nine
Frankie

The sun had set by the time Pegasus soared over London and down towards Asfaleia House. The night sky was full of stars again, and I could sworn the constellation Seb pointed out as Herakles was winking at us as we flew past. Pegasus hit the ground running, coming to a stop outside the stables.

"You'd better hop off here," Pegasus said. "I can't have Bill seeing my wings."

We jumped down and watched as Pegasus made his way towards the stables, his wings tucked in against him.

"How does Bill not notice the wings?" Clara asked.

"I might have something to do with that," Zeus smirked. "But I couldn't possibly say."

We walked together towards the House, each of us letting our armour fall off us as we did. Zeus was beaming from ear to ear.

"Home," he smiled, leading us up into the House. Hephaestus' rooms were still baking hot as we marched past, and Demeter's still smelt of freshly-cut flowers. From Poseidon's rooms came the rush of seawater, and I saw Zeus shudder as he heard it.

"Ready?" Zeus asked, as we made it to the heavy door that led into the War Room where we had first met the gods. From inside, we could hear the shouts that made it clear that the gods were mid-argument.

"Ready." we smiled back at Zeus.

Together, four mortals and one god pushed open the door.

"They are obviously dead," Hera was saying. "I knew it was pointless, sending three mortals out there to look for Zeus! And as for the one Thanatos took over—"

"If you're so sure they're dead," Hades answered, "then maybe you can explain why they haven't arrived in the Underworld!"

"You're the King of the Dead!" Hera shot back, "maybe you should be wondering why your subjects aren't arriving before you!"

"Or perhaps," Zeus bellowed, cutting them both off. "They have not arrived in the Underworld because they succeed in their quest and are in fact alive?"

"Well, I don't see," Hera began, not looking up, "what proof anyone in this room has to prove they're alive!"

"Mother," Hephaestus said, smirking at us from under his beard. "Perhaps you should look up."

"Hm," Hera sniffed, raising her eyes. "ZEUS? You're alive!" she exclaimed, leaping out of her seat.

"It would appear so, dear wife," Zeus smiled.

The roar that went up from the gods was deafening. They were on their feet, hollering and whooping as Zeus made his way around the table, embracing them all. Even Hades got a hug.

"Where were you?" Apollo and Artemis asked together.

"Was it a terribly dangerous quest?" asked Demeter worriedly.

"What happened to Thanatos?" asked Aphrodite.

"What battle plan did you use?" chipped in Athena.

"Did you pulverise anyone?" asked Ares.

"Was there wine?" slurred Dionysus, drunkenly.

"Silence, silence." Zeus laughed, taking his seat at the head of the table. "I shall answer all your questions in time, my family. But first, we must thank our mortal friends who found me!"

"Hm," sniffed Hera. "And how can we be sure that they

211

found you?"

"Quite easily, my darling wife," Zeus crooned. "You must take my word for it. And as my word is law, you have no choice."

Hera scowled. She really didn't like us.

"As I was saying, we must honour them! Not only did they find me, but they also single handily fought off two of the fiercest Primordial Deities we have faced!"

None of us thought to correct him about that. Hades was grinning at us.

"Tell me, family, what honours can we bestow?" Zeus asked.

"We could give them the honour of a noble death at my hands," Ares offered. We shrank away from him.

"I don't think so, no," said Zeus. "But thank you for the offer, Ares. Anyone else have a suggestion?"

"Perhaps," said Aphrodite, sweeping her hair out of her face, "we could give them makeovers!"

"Another hard pass I am afraid, Aphrodite. They are already far too beautiful," Zeus said with a smile.

"How about we ask them what they want?" Hades said, as if it was the easiest answer to give.

"What a good idea," smiled Zeus. "What would you like?"

"Nothing," Seb said. "Except maybe a cab to take us home."

"And maybe some fighting lessons with Artemis," I said.

"And, if it's ok, maybe some sailing lessons from Poseidon?" Levi put in.

"And some music lessons from Apollo?" Clara said.

Zeus let out a long laugh. "You don't ask for much, do you?" he chuckled. "But I can't think of a reason not to grant you these wishes!"

We all grinned at one another.

Maybe getting to know the gods would have its advantages after all.

Chapter Thirty
Seb

Zeus had been as good as his word. He'd arranged for a normal, mortal cab to drive us all home, and had promised to be in touch regarding our other requests. We'd seen Clara and Levi off home, and now Frankie and I were stood outside her house.

"Did any of that really happen?" she asked, as the cab pulled away.

"I think so," I said. It had been a week since we'd snuck into Demeter's shop and had our lives turned upside down. "I hope so."

"Do you think we'll ever see the gods again?" Frankie asked hopefully.

"I don't know," I said. I wanted to. I really, really, really wanted to. We'd had the kind of adventure most people only dream about, and now it felt like it was being snatched away from us.

"Come on," Frankie said, pulling me towards the door. "We'd better go in."

The Sibanda's house looked exactly the same as when we'd last been in it. Rosie and Raf were cuddled up on the sofa making puppy-dog eyes at one another, Mr Sibanda was still talking about the new car he wanted to buy, and Mum and Ma were chatting to Mrs Sibanda about her florist business.

"Oh, I took it over when the old boss retired," Mrs Sibanda was saying. Me and Frankie grinned at one another. There was no mention of a business partner who was secretly a Greek

213

goddess. Whatever enchantments the gods had placed on our families to make them believe we'd been on a school trip, it had worked. Ma had explained that there had been a letter posted to all the parents of students in the school yesterday explaining that, due to family issues, Mrs Pallas and Mr Crawford would be leaving with immediate effect. I'd had to stifle a laugh at that. The gods had some of the biggest family issues around, after all.

"How was your trip?" asked Mr Sibanda, looking up from his car magazine.

"Boring," Frankie and I said at the same time.

After all, it's not like we saved the King of the Gods or anything, was it?

Epilogue
Antigone

I don't know where I am.

After Zeus took care of Thanatos my cave began to crumble again, and Erebus had been stood in front of me.

"You have done well," he said. "But the plan must advance. Thanatos has been defeated, and the gods will begin their fight back against me and my kind. It is time, Antigone, for you to fulfil your role in my plans."

He had said something in Ancient Greek and the next thing I knew I was falling backwards and forwards until I landed with a thump outside what looked like the sort of place people in Greece would have gone to prove their strength. Herakles was stood in front of me.

"Did they suspect anything?" he asked, his brow sweating and his hair stuck to his head.

"Nothing," I said.

"Good," said Herakles. "Lord Erebus has plans for you, Antigone. I fulfilled my role by acting as a spy. Now you must fulfil yours. You must lure those four mortals into a trap. You will be the one to remove them from the gods and leave them stranded. Go, Antigone. Find them. And bring about their destruction."

The End... For Now